$20.00   05-1209
M   Irvine, R. R.
Irv.. Ratings are
R.   murder.

Ratings Are Murder

Also by R. R. Irvine

Bob Christopher Mysteries
Horizontal Hold
Freeze Frame
Jump Cut

other novels
The Devil's Breath
Footsteps
The Face Out Front

Ratings Are Murder

R. R. Irvine

ASBURY PARK PUBLIC LIBRARY
ASBURY PARK NEW JERSEY

Walker and Company
New York

Copyright © 1985 by Robert R. Irvine

All right reserved. No part of this book may be reproduced or transmitted in any form or by any means, electric or mechanical, including photocopying, recording, or by any information storage and retrieval system, without permission in writing from the Publisher.

All the characters and events portrayed in this story are fictitious.

First published in the United States of America in 1985 by the Walker Publishing Company, Inc.

Published simultaneously in Canada by John Wiley & Sons Canada, Limited, Rexdale, Ontario.

Library of Congress Cataloging in Publication Data

Irvine, R. R. (Robert R.)
   Ratings are murder.

   I. Title.
PS3559.R65R3   1985   813'.54   84-29931
ISBN 0-8027-5620-4

Book Design by Teresa M. Carboni

Printed in the United States of America

10 9 8 7 6 5 4 3 2 1

To Jon L. Breen

1

"YOUR MONEY OR your life," shouted the masked bandit, pressing a gun to Bob Christopher's nose. The robber was wearing an old-fashioned duster and a bedraggled Stetson from which rain sluiced in a torrent.

Christopher, his hands full, tried side-stepping but more "Wheeler-Dealers" closed around him, among them Babe Ruth, Winnie the Pooh, and a Mae West look-alike real enough to put a pistol in your pocket.

All things being equal, contestants for the thirty minutes of avarice called "Wheeler-Dealers" that followed the news each night on Channel 3 were selected on the basis of how original their costumes were. Of course, the show's producers also took into account those indefinables they liked to call "personality," otherwise known as bosoms and hairy chests.

"For God's sake," Christopher muttered, "can't you see I'm in a hurry?"

Paying no attention, the "Wheeler-Dealers" plucked at him eagerly. He shuddered, and the stack of video tape cassettes he was sheltering under his raincoat teetered dangerously. If they got wet, he would lose the tornado story.

The bandit cocked his gun, real enough looking to make Christopher wince.

"Don't ya recognize Jesse James when ya see 'im?"

"Me and everybody else," Christopher snapped irritably. He didn't have time for "Wheeler-Dealers" today. In fact, if he didn't get moving there'd be no hope of finding a tape editor.

"Whaddya mean?" A whine had crept into the bandit's voice.

"We ran the old Tyrone Power movie about Jesse last week. Ever since, he's been a glut on the game show market."

"I'm *Frank* James," the man said hastily.

Christopher shook his head, momentarily dislodging the gun.

"Billy the Kid?"

"I'm not the one you have to convince."

The masked man withdrew the weapon far enough to take a threatening bead on Christopher. "Don't try putting anything over on me. I've seen you on the tube."

"Maybe on the news."

"You're not Bill Bowzer?"

Now there was a compliment to draw blood. Bowzer, though handsome enough to grab rating points, was "Wheeler-Dealers" 's host.

"I'm Robert Christopher."

Jesse James swore, then popped the six-shooter into his mouth and pulled the trigger. His cheeks lit up. The gun was a flashlight.

Suddenly someone in the crowd shouted, "There he is!"

The resulting stampede sent Christopher reeling.

"Here's Billy the Kid!" hollered the former Jesse James, and sprinted off toward Bowzer, who stood with his arms outspread, welcoming his flock like a pontiff giving benediction.

Insanity, Christopher thought, righting himself and staggering toward the tech building. Here he was with tape footage of the biggest story to hit Los Angeles all year, and he had to fight his way through people with nothing more on their minds than getting something for nothing. If he were ever put in charge of a television station like Channel 3, especially one sharing facilities with its mother network, he'd build a wall around the news department. Outsiders trying to climb over it would be shot on sight.

The technical building, like most other structures on the old movie lot, had all the permanency of an army barracks. Even so, the flimsy door was more than Christopher could handle without exposing his video tapes to the downpour. His struggles caused him to lose control of the cassettes, forcing him to go down on his knees to save them from a dunking.

He landed in a puddle. He didn't dare move for fear of wetting his hoard. All he could do was bang his head against the door until someone came to his rescue. That someone was just the man Christopher wanted to see, Fat Jack Pollard, the shift supervisor.

"We've got an emergency," Christopher began as soon as Fat Jack gave him a hand with the tapes.

"So who hasn't?" Fat Jack answered as he led the way to his office.

"This is the worst storm in years. We've got crews all over town. I'm on deadline and every tape editor in the news department is tied up."

"So you've come to me."

"Can you spare someone?"

"Your boss called to ask me the same thing not two minutes ago."

"What did you tell *him*?"

"The same thing I'll tell you. I've got an extra man, but he's not here yet. He's late. So what else is new?"

"Don't tell me."

"You guessed it. Bingo Bradford's your man."

As a featured reporter on "The Six O'Clock News," Christopher was assigned an editor on a regular basis. But during emergencies, such as now, potluck was the rule. Hearing Bingo Bradford's name meant Christopher's luck had just gone to pot.

"When was he due in?"

"He ought to be here soon," Fat Jack answered, unwilling to give out specifics. "Why don't you get yourself a cup of coffee while you wait?"

3

Christopher put down his tapes and glanced at the clock on the wall. He had two hours until air. With an editor like Bingo, that would be cutting it close.

"Can't you give me someone else?"

"It's Bingo or nothing."

Just then the elusive Bingo, so soaking wet that his Dodgers' cap was bleeding blue, tried to sneak himself and his film cans past the shift supervisor. But Fat Jack had seen that move before. He shoved Christopher to one side and leapt out of his cubbyhole office, grabbing Bingo in a bear hug. Cans went flying, one of them rolling noisily toward the editing rooms at the other end of the hall.

"You're an hour late!" Fat Jack shouted.

Bingo struggled to break the hug but he was no match for the two-hundred-and-fifty-pound supervisor.

"My film!" Bingo pleaded.

Fat Jack relented, unlocking his arms. Instantly Bingo fell on hands and knees to retrieve his treasures. He didn't seem to notice that one had gotten away.

Scooping up the errant can, Christopher said, "I'll make you a trade, Bingo. Your body for this film."

"Just give me a couple of minutes with him," Fat Jack said, "and he's all yours."

"Give me a break," Bingo begged. "Not *Christopher*." The tape editor, who was about as sensitive as an Arab terrorist, spoke as though the reporter wasn't there. "Anybody but him."

Fat Jack shook his head. "In case you haven't noticed, we've got a big story on our hands."

Bingo raised his eyes skyward as if seeking the rain, which had been coming down steadily for five days, dumping more than two inches of water on Los Angeles every twenty-four hours.

"I've had it with you," the shift supervisor announced. He, too, ignored the reporter's presence.

"Relax, Jack. We can talk later. Right now, it's costing me money not to punch in."

The video tape supervisor snorted. "Since when? You

know I covered for you. Your time card says you were here right on the dot. But that's it. From now on you don't get so much as a coffee break. Christopher here has you for the next eight hours."

Bingo pulled his sopping cap down further over his eyes. His fingers came away blue. "I promised to get these films transferred to tape today. Otherwise—"

With a curse, Fat Jack cut Bingo off, herding him back against the wall of the tiny office. "Let's not broadcast our business for everyone to hear. Your dubs are going to have to wait."

"I thought we had an arrangement."

"We do. But this has nothing to do with it."

Christopher knew from past encounters about the sweetheart deals these two had. In return for two hours of unworked overtime each day, the tape editor turned a blind eye on debts incurred by Fat Jack in Bingo's bingo game, which ran nightly during the union-specified meal break.

Fat Jack rubbed his neck. "You have to cool it today. That's all there is to it."

"Can we get to work now?" Christopher said. "I'm on the air at six."

Bingo paid no attention. He banged a couple of cans together. "Do you know what these films are, Jack?"

"I don't want to know."

"Classics, that's what. Twenty years old I'm told, but hot stuff even by today's standards."

"Pornography is pornography."

"I've got collectors standing in line."

"And reporters," Christopher reminded him.

"Why do you have to give him me?" Bingo asked, glaring at his supervisor.

"Because I covered the twister," Christopher explained. "That's got priority. And right now you're the only editor available."

"Christopher's an old lady," Bingo moaned.

The tape supervisor leaned up against the wall and shifted

his bulky back as if he had an itch he couldn't reach. "And one more thing, Bingo. The tape loss around here is getting out of hand. From now on you're going to have to buy your own."

Sputtering obscenities, Bingo stalked down the hall and through the sliding glass door to his editing room. Christopher stayed right with him.

The editing cubicle, no more than six by eight feet, was a maze of electronic gear. There were half a dozen TV monitors, a computer, videotape recorders, amplifiers, turntables, audio decks, oscilloscopes and a patch-bay similar in appearance to a bank of old-fashioned telephone switchboards. That bay enabled Bingo to plug into any other facility on the American Broadcasting Network lot. He could receive output from sound stages and recording studios; he could even transmit. But at the moment he was slamming things around, feigning technical difficulties. Christopher knew that dodge. He waited the man out.

Finally Bingo settled down in front of the computer console that controlled video tape editing. From then on he spoke only in grunts, which suited Christopher, who kept his instructions to a minimum. As a result, they reached the final tornado edit with thirty minutes to spare.

For the first time, Christopher could think ahead to his script. Out loud, he began rehearsing possible openings for his story, which was certain to be the lead item on "The Six O'Clock News."

Grimacing, Bingo glanced up from the editing computer and said, "Good God, Christopher, your tongue's green."

The reporter's mouth snapped shut. He opened it just enough to swear before rushing down the hall to check himself in the men's room mirror.

Sure enough. His tongue was disgusting. That damned diet of his was to blame. The "studio diet," it was called. It should have been named after George Washington, or some other President whose picture appeared on money. It was making enough for its creator, who said calories didn't count as long as you ate only foods that were green.

Christopher pounded the mirror with his fist. Sometimes he wondered if he shouldn't go into another line of work, one where cameras didn't distort a man's waistline.

Making disgusting noises, he washed out his mouth with liquid soap. But his tongue remained a bilious green.

He clenched his teeth. On the air tonight he'd have to speak like a ventriloquist.

Keeping his mouth shut, he hurried back to the editing room. It was empty. Christopher shouted for Bingo, but there was no answer.

The reporter rushed along the carpeted corridor, peering into each cubicle as he went. There was no sign of Bingo, no one Christopher even recognized until he reached the last room before Fat Jack's office. Here he found Father John, advisor to Channel 3's one religious show, "Vision."

"Have you seen Bingo Bradford?" he asked.

The priest stepped out of the cubicle. "He was here just a minute ago, but he left in a rush. I think he went outside."

"That bastard was trying to scrounge some of our video tapes," said a voice from inside the editing room.

Christopher poked his head through the cubicle's open doorway. The other two members of the "Vision" crew, producer Robin Flick and technical director Svend Yoder, were there.

"Bingo was trying to steal tape for his sex shows," Yoder said, smiling apologetically at the priest. As usual, the TD was outspoken. Past candor had buried him on the station's religious concession to license renewal. As such "Vision" was condemned to the ghetto of Sunday morning television, with a 6:30 A.M. time slot that guaranteed an audience so small the rating service couldn't even measure it.

"I was just going for coffee," Father John said. "Can I get you a cup, Bob?"

Christopher's deadline was closing in, but there wasn't

much he could do until Bingo returned. As a last resort, he could have Svend pull the tape from Bingo's machine without making the final edit. Union regulations prevented the reporter from touching so much as a knob on any of the equipment himself. In fact, Christopher decided to do that right now and save a lot of worry.

"Happy to," Yoder told him, "if my producer doesn't object."

Robin's shrug of indifference failed to mask her irritation at being interrupted. She was young, pretty, and so well dressed that she radiated ambition enough to kill a Geiger counter.

As soon as the TD stepped into Bingo's editing room he stopped dead in his tracks and pointed at the floor. "There's water in here."

"Bingo was all wet when we started," Christopher explained. "So was I for that matter."

"It's a goddamn lake." Yoder spit in the puddle that was already up over the carpet's nap. Then he pointed to the wall behind the patch-bay. Leaking water was cascading down the masonry. "I'm not going in there, not without rubber boots."

"Just get my tape. That's all I'm asking."

The TD took a tentative step onto the squishy carpet. "And take a look at that." He was waving at the patch-bay. "Bingo's got lines plugged in all over this lot. There's one to projection. One to local editing. Shit. He's got enough volts running through this place to fry us where we stand."

Yoder went up on tiptoe. "If I'm any judge, he's hooked up to half a dozen recording studios at least. He must be going into the wholesale porno business."

"Coffee," Father John called from the other end of the hall.

"Saved," the TD said and retreated.

Christopher cast a longing glance at the cassette containing his tornado footage. So close, yet so far away.

Once inserted into a machine, cassettes became the domain of the technical unions. To touch it now could trigger sanctions anywhere from a fine to a strike. So, with a weary sigh, he left his story behind and rejoined the others.

The priest handed him a styrofoam cup that leaked. Christopher scalded his tongue before asking, "What brings you people here so early?" Production on "Vision" was usually confined to the dead hours after midnight.

"A cancellation," Yoder said. "Otherwise, we'd never see the light of day."

"We're trying to create a new opening for our show," Robin said impatiently.

"What's wrong with the old one?" Christopher asked, though he couldn't remember what it looked like.

"Nothing," Father John answered, "especially if you're as partial to stained glass windows as I am."

Robin sighed. "We've been over this before. The program director wants us to do something more spectacular, something to boost our ratings."

The TD snorted derisively. "Nobody but a zealot is going to watch us anyway. No offense, Father. But that's the way it is Sunday mornings. Now if we had religious cartoons . . ."

"I hardly think His Eminence would give approval to something like that," the priest replied.

"There you have it then," Yoder announced. "There's no way to jazz up a show like this."

"Sweeps are coming right up," Robin countered.

Sweeps was one of the few things that could kill Christopher's appetite. When sweeps week arrived, journalism vanished from the news, replaced by exposés on prostitution, the newest venereal diseases, gay love, anything sexual to hype the ratings.

The TD swore.

Three times a year the rating services canvass the entire country, the top 155 television markets—a clean *sweep*,

9

so to speak. At the end of each sweep period, a rating book is issued. Those results determine the price of the station's commercials for the next quarter.

Father John spoke soothingly. "It won't hurt to have a look at what Robin has in mind."

Her only acknowledgment of the priest's support was a curt nod. "I've dug out some old film footage shot at a local passion play. It's already in projection."

Angrily Yoder hit the talk-back switch and ordered a film-chain readied for playback.

A moment later film rolled. Numbers flashed by on one of the TV monitors in their cubicle. Without transition, a robed Christ filled the screen, arms outstretched as he walked slowly toward camera. Viewed without accompanying sound, the actor looked stiff and amateurish, like someone in a home movie.

Yoder jeered. Father John sighed.

Finally, at Robin's urging, the TD tried superimposing Christ over the regular opening, a panorama of stained-glass windows. When that didn't improve matters, he began experimenting with special effects, fading the figure in and out. At one point Christ turned into something resembling a ghost.

Suddenly the savior was surrounded by naked, copulating bodies.

"Sacrilege," muttered Father John.

Yoder slapped several talk-back keys at the same time, while screaming, "Bingo, you bastard!" The TD kept throwing switches and punching buttons, but to no effect. Christ continued to float through the orgy.

Yoder slammed his fist on the console in front of him. The impact did something. The religious film hung up in the projector and began to burn.

Father John crossed himself.

Christopher hurled his coffee cup into a trashcan and sprinted down the hall. At the doorway to Bingo's cubicle, the reporter skidded to an abrupt halt, gaping at his tape editor in disbelief.

10

Water ran from Bingo's sopping baseball cap, his jeans and his shirt, while Dodger-blue tinted the growing puddle in which he knelt. His every movement produced squishing sounds, unnaturally loud in the confines of the tiny editing room. There was the smell of something burning, something electrical.

A screech came over the talk-back speaker.

"Lord, it's me," Bingo said. "Bingo Barchiesi. I'm sorry. I should never have changed my name. Mother warned me you couldn't find me if I changed it. 'God is an Italian,' she said, 'and now He won't know where to look for you.' "

The editor's shaking legs stirred waves so high they lapped at the base of the patch-bay.

"Bingo!" a voiced boomed over the talk-back.

"Yes, Lord."

"Dammit, Bingo. I know you're there."

From where he stood, Christopher saw the editor's eyes roll up until nothing showed but white.

"You idiot. You've short-circuited half the equipment on this lot."

Christopher recognized Yoder's voice. And so apparently did Bingo, whose eyes reappeared, immediately coming to rest on the reporter. Recognition brought the editor up on his feet. He swore, then began pulling plugs from the patch-bay. The orgy disappeared from the monitors.

"Did you see that, Bob?"

"What?"

"Jesus Christ. He came to me, there on the screen." A trembling hand waved at the bank of TV screens.

"They're working on 'Vision' down the hall."

"You mean that wasn't . . ." Bingo swallowed whatever else he was about to say.

"Somehow their film got mixed with yours. I just pray to God that you haven't screwed up my tornado tape."

"How much of my film did you see?"

"A few seconds." Christopher grinned. "Quit worrying. The only person you shocked was Father John."

11

"Did you see any familiar faces?" Bingo demanded.

"What the hell do you mean?"

"You know, on my film."

"I saw naked people."

"No faces?"

"It wasn't their faces I was looking at."

Bingo squinted suspiciously. "You did see it, didn't you?" He shook a fist at the reporter.

Christopher swallowed to keep from laughing.

"If you keep it to yourself," Bingo pleaded, lowering his voice, "there's more than enough money in this for two. He'll have to pay plenty to keep us quiet."

Pirating pornography was one thing, but suddenly Bingo sounded suspiciously like a blackmailer.

"That kind of thing can get you killed," Christopher said. "Besides—"

A hissing sound filled the editing room. Smoke erupted from the patch-bay.

Terror distorted Bingo's face. "We'll be electrocuted," he gasped. With that, he leapt for dry carpet, then kept right on going down the hall and out the door.

Risking electrocution and, worse, a union walk out, Christopher waded inside the smoke-filled cubicle to rescue his videotape.

2

THE APPARITION APPEARED out of nowhere. One moment Christopher was alone in the newsroom typing his notes; in the next he looked up to see her standing in the doorway. Backlit, with her features hidden in shadow, she seemed to radiate sensuality. But as she stepped into the light, he saw that she was an old woman, her expression fixed like someone possessed.

With a sharp expulsion of breath, the reporter leapt to his feet. This late at night, with "The Eleven O'Clock News" long gone, he wasn't taking any chances. Lunatics did manage to slip past the guards occasionally.

"St. Christopher," she whispered.

The reporter shook his head; he probably hadn't heard correctly.

"I'm the cleaning woman," she explained, though the way she held her body suggested something far more provocative. "Irma O'Donnell."

He smiled sheepishly. He recognized her now, a late-night fixture around the studio. Until a moment ago, when she suddenly appeared in the doorway, he had never noticed that she had the figure of someone much younger. Up close, however, there was no hiding the wrinkles and limp gray hair. Only her eyes seemed young, shining as they were.

"I watch you every night on the news," she said.

He nodded stiffly, not quite certain how to respond.

Cord-like muscles stood out in her neck. Being a cleaning woman didn't guarantee sanity, he decided, wondering where the overnight security man had gotten to. For that matter, Christopher's cameraman ought to be around someplace. In the news director's office making unauthorized long-distance phone calls, no doubt.

"I saw your report on the tornado," Irma said. "It surprised me."

Christopher sighed. The old woman was turning out to be a critic, not a lunatic. That, at least, was the kind of thing he knew how to deal with.

"I thought you were a consumer reporter," she said accusingly.

"That used to be my full-time assignment. But these days my role is expanding. Besides, with weather like this everyone pitches in."

"How long will you be tied up on the storm?"

Her tone of voice changed, became cajoling, almost as if she was flirting with him.

"It depends," he answered, backing up a step. "If the assignment desk needs me, I've got to remain available. That's why I'm here so late."

He tapped his watch. It was midnight. He would have been home long ago except for the hour wasted chasing Bingo around the lot to get a second report prepared for "The Eleven O'Clock News."

"You help people in trouble," she said, closing the gap between them. "I've seen you."

She reached out to touch him. Christopher stepped out of the way.

"But I guess no one can help me." Irma lowered her head as if she was suddenly too shy to look him in the face. After a moment she peeked up at him and smiled, her eyelashes fluttering. It was a girlish gesture, one he found somewhat repulsive coming from a woman her age.

"If you can't help me," she said, "nobody can." Her voice had dropped so low that Christopher found himself leaning forward to catch her last words.

She touched him. "Saint Christopher," she breathed. She fished a medal from inside her sweater. "The patron saint of travelers," she said, holding out the medallion so that the reporter could see the silver image. "My patron saint, too. Only he isn't really a saint anymore."

For a moment, he didn't know what she meant. Then he remembered that the Catholic church had withdrawn Christopher's sainthood sometime during the sixties. He couldn't recall why.

"Everybody says you take up lost causes," Irma went on.

"I manage to win some," the reporter said. He didn't know if he liked the reputation he was building or not. But he did have to admit a distinct affinity for underdogs.

"Can you win one for me?"

Had he heard Irma speak that last line over the phone, he would have thought she was a young girl.

"Win what?" he asked.

"Oh, I thought you understood. I want you to help me get Saint Christopher reinstated."

The reporter clenched his teeth.

"I've already written to the Pope, several times."

"And what does *he* say?"

"Someone else answered for him. It was a nice note, on official Vatican stationery and everything, but it didn't help. The church says there isn't any real proof that Saint Christopher ever existed. Imagine that." She clutched her medal with both hands. "I can feel his power."

Christopher looked away.

"You're his namesake," she pleaded.

Before he could reply, the overnight man, Hap Taylor, returned. "I've been in the can," he shouted across the newsroom. "Any calls?"

"I don't know," Christopher answered. In the news business, answering phones could be hazardous any time of the day. But during the dead hours, lunatics dialed with a vengeance. So Christopher made it a rule to go deaf after the late news.

Taylor bellowed an obscenity before returning to his desk, where he began sorting through the yards of wire copy that had accumulated in his absence.

During the overnight man's interruption, Christopher had tried to think of a way to let the old lady down easy, even though he had learned a long time ago that a straight rejection was often best. Anything else might raise false hopes.

She blinked her mascaraed lashes at him. All at once her real intention became clear to him. She wanted the attention of a man, a younger man. And he was it. Perhaps watching him on the tube had triggered some kind of fantasy for her.

Taking a deep breath, Christopher prepared to say no.

That was when Taylor exploded. He stomped over to the reporter's desk. "Didn't you hear the bells, Christopher? Two bulletins in the last ten minutes. Another tornado touched down." The overnight man looked to Irma for sympathy. But she was occupied with her medal.

Taylor turned his attention back to Christopher. "We'll need a crew on the scene for the morning news inserts. Lucky you're still here."

"I've been out in the rain all day," Christopher said.

"Are you refusing an assignment?"

"I'm here, aren't I? If I don't go, you'll have to get someone else out of bed. I don't want that on my conscience."

"You're too soft," Taylor said. "Now where's your cameraman gotten to?"

"In Reisner's office, I think."

The overnight man left the newsroom and returned a moment later with John Fitzgerald, Christopher's cameraman and close friend.

Irma, meanwhile, had moved back out of the way, perching on one of the larger desks. The maneuver exposed her slender legs. Black stockings camouflaged any blemishes of age.

"Now, all I need is a soundman," Taylor announced. "Floyd Scanlon is your other half, isn't he Fitzgerald?"

"He'll love you," the cameraman answered. "This will mean a call-back, plus overtime—for both of us."

"I'm not calling you back from anywhere," Taylor complained. "You're already here."

"I'm on my own time. You're a union man. You know the rules."

"My union isn't worth spit. Otherwise the news director wouldn't be able to do this to me. Have you ever tried working midnight to eight? You can't sleep when you get home because the birds are singing their lousy heads off. I'm telling you . . ."

Abruptly Taylor's thin, sharp face took on a sly look. He rubbed his hands together. "According to Reisner's rules, he can be called at home any time of the day or night for a bona fide emergency. A tornado certainly ought to qualify, don't you think?"

When Christopher and Fitzgerald agreed, the overnight man trotted off to use his own phone.

"No wonder he never sees the light of day," the cameraman muttered. He looked questioningly at the cleaning woman.

"This is Irma O'Donnell," the reporter explained.

"You're sitting on a shrine," Fitzgerald told her. "That's Al Aarons's desk."

Irma jumped as if she'd actually committed a sacrilege.

"Let me show you how gods and anchormen live," Fitzgerald said. He bent over the desk and tried to open a side drawer. "He's locking it again." With that the cameraman rummaged in his pocket, pulled out a penknife, and began to jimmy the lock.

After a few moments, Fitzgerald began looking around the newsroom for something better than his knife. The room itself was a large bullpen, some fifty feet long and maybe half that across, designed to look good as an on-camera backdrop to the news while also functioning as a work area. Utility, however, had been sacrificed to the needs of lighting directors and set planners. As a result, reporters' desks, like Christopher's, were crammed together along one windowless wall. Anchormen, however, had space enough to play shuffleboard on the expanse of red carpet surrounding their desks. Hap Taylor's domain, the assignment area, stood in one corner, encircled by wire machines, radios, and scanners monitoring police and fire frequencies.

Separating the newsroom from the on-air studio was a floor-to-ceiling plexiglass wall, supposedly soundproof. But anything above a whisper was strictly forbidden during broadcasts.

"Here we go," the cameraman announced as he returned with a letter opener. He had the drawer open in seconds.

"Now," Fitzgerald said, donning Al Aarons's spare toupee, "how do I look?"

Irma only shook her head. Fitzgerald examined himself in the mirror that Aarons kept in the same drawer. Then the cameraman drew himself up to his full six-foot, six-inch height and dramatically proclaimed, "A little hair of the dog."

"That kind of remark got Hap Taylor sentenced to the overnight," Christopher said.

"I've got better union protection." The cameraman's laugh was so infectious that even Irma smiled. Fitzgerald often had that kind of effect on people. With his Irish charm and good looks, he resembled the late President Kennedy, with whom he shared two names. Only at Channel 3, they didn't call their John "Jack." They called him "F-Stop" Fitzgerald.

Hap Taylor whooped triumphantly. "Reisner's coming in to supervise the storm coverage himself. I'll have company in my suffering." The overnight man clapped his hands. "By the way, Scanlon says he'll be here in thirty minutes."

"That means an hour," F-Stop said. "You know Floyd. He'll stop to eat first."

Irma interrupted. "Mr. Christopher, how soon will you be leaving?"

"As soon as our soundman arrives."

"Could I speak to you alone first?"

With a sigh, Christopher nodded to his cameraman. "Maybe we ought to have something to eat ourselves."

"I'll see what I can fish out of the machines," F-Stop said before trotting away.

"We can use the news director's office," Christopher told her. He led the way.

Reisner's office was spacious, with enough room for a long leather couch and a glass-topped conference table surrounded by four uncomfortable chairs. On the wall behind the veneered desk was a hand-carved wooden plaque that read THINK MEAN.

As Christopher and Irma sat facing one another across the glass expanse, the reporter readied himself to get rid of her. Even under the best of circumstances, a consumer advocate was up against terrible odds. But taking on the Catholic church didn't bear thinking about. Assuming, of course, that the old girl was in her right mind.

"You're the perfect namesake," Irma said.

Christopher hesitated, searching for the right words. Even a looney old lady deserved common courtesy.

Before he could speak, she reached out timidly and took his hand. This time he didn't resist.

"I saw him, you know, just like I see you every night."

"Who?"

"St. Christopher of course. He showed himself to me, on TV when I was cleaning the news set."

"When did this happen?"

"Just before 'The Six O'Clock News.'"

"Uh-huh," Christopher muttered. "And what did he look like?"

"Like a saint of course. He wore a long white robe and his arms were reaching out, beckoning to me. I knew it was a sign. I knew what he wanted me to do."

"And what was that?"

"Just like I told you. Get him reinstated. With your help, of course."

She'd had a vision all right, thanks to Bingo's short-circuiting.

19

"And what else did you see?"

"Myself. The evil that all of us have within us."

That translated into Bingo's pornography. He was about to explain that when she went on. "I have sinned." The little-girl voice was gone now. "And I have to pay for it."

She grasped her silver medallion and began to cry. "I'm afraid."

The reporter stared into her face, looking for fear. What he saw was too much make-up and running mascara.

"When I decided to come to you, I knew there would be no turning back . . . that I might have to pay with my life."

Now he knew she was crazy. But then half the people he knew in television were paranoid, fearing that their careers would be murdered at any moment.

"I was warned," she added.

She stopped speaking then, drying her eyes with a crumpled tissue that she pulled from the sleeve of her sweater.

"I'd like to help you, but . . ." The reporter shrugged helplessly.

"He'll know I've been to see you."

"Who, St. Christopher?"

She shook her head solemnly. "Oh, no. Not St. Christopher. But I don't mind, not after talking to you."

"I don't understand."

Irma wiped away the last of her mascara. She looked ancient now, and shrunken. No sign of lost youth.

"You're my St. Christopher. He can't take that away from me, even if he kills me."

Christopher sighed. Even Al Aarons wasn't this paranoid. "Who would want to kill you?" he asked softly.

"If you can get my saint reinstated, maybe I'll be saved, too." Without warning she clasped both hands over her Christopher medal and fell to her knees, as though praying. "You have helped me already. My fear is fading."

A gleam had come back into her eyes. As a newsman he'd seen it before. Charlie Manson had it. Sirhan too. Fanatics who saw their own kind of reality.

If Irma belonged in *that* category, she would cling to her own vision, no matter what. All Christopher could say was, "I'll look into it." It wasn't a lie. He'd have one of the researchers look up St. Christopher. Maybe he'd even send along a copy of the results to Irma.

"Promise?" she asked.

He didn't care to go quite that far, so he answered with a smile. She didn't seem to notice the difference.

"One more thing," she said. "I can pay you."

"That won't be necessary."

"Don't be fooled just because I'm a cleaning woman. I was an actress once." She chuckled. "Now I've been getting regular bonuses—from the station."

"For your acting?"

"That's for me to know, isn't it?"

Christopher was intrigued. "If you want my help, you'll have to be honest with me."

"It's money to keep me quiet," she said.

"About what?"

"Not now, not until I have my St. Christopher back."

"But . . ."

Irma took his hand and kissed it. That was the moment when Herb Reisner arrived. He took one look at them and said, "Out!" Then he pointed to the THINK MEAN sign on the wall. "I don't want anything immoral going on in my office."

"You're all bluff, Herb," the reporter said.

But Irma fled, the back of her neck suddenly bright red. As soon as the door closed behind her, the news director grabbed the reporter's arm and asked, "What was that all about?"

"I'm not really sure. Maybe she isn't so crazy."

"She kissed your hand, for God's sake."

Absently, Christopher stared down at the lipstick mark Irma had left.

"Forget it. We've got things to do before your soundman arrives." Reisner paused to stretch out on his couch. "I want you to cut some three-second teases. We'll sandwich them throughout the all-night movies, promoting our 11 A.M. news."

"Can't you get me a little more time than that?"

"The commercials and public service spots have already been programmed into the computer. The three-second breaks are slopovers really. We'll be lucky to jam in teases without screwing up the timing."

"Just what do you have in mind?"

Reisner closed his eyes. After a moment he smiled and said, "Tornado terror. Film at Eleven."

Christopher merely nodded. Normally he would have objected to such sensationalism, but at the moment his attention was consumed by an old woman with a girl's figure and voice. An old woman in search of a saint.

"Christopher canonized," he retorted. "Film at eleven."

3

CROSSING THE ABN studio lot the next day, Christopher felt anything but saintly. Hellish would be more like it. Wind-whipped rain half blinded him, though not enough to disguise the fact that the shelter of the news building was still a hundred yards away. Before reaching its sanctuary, he'd have to cross the land of network make-believe, presently populated by hard-core fans milling beneath the corrugated metal roof of the audience holding area.

He started to run, but a sudden intensified downpour forced him to take shelter with the audience, who were huddled in a tight knot and protected only by a corrugated metal roof. Walls were considered an unnecessary expense in Southern California where, so the song lyrics said, it never rained.

Christopher immediately found himself sandwiched among the faithful, hearty souls with murder on their minds.

"Sister Angela left the convent because she killed Mother Superior."

"No. She left to marry Jason."

"By then she already knew he was a homosexual living with another man."

"It was because of Jason's lover that Angela went through with the ceremony."

"She got herself pregnant by him."

"I felt terrible about the baby though. When it died, I knew it was a sign for Angela to devote the rest of her life to good deeds."

"If she hadn't become a nurse at Emergency Hospital, she wouldn't have met Peter."

"Surgeons give me the creeps."

"Angela should have known better than to fall for one.

He's going to commit another murder this afternoon, you know. *TV Guide* says so."

"Ooo! There he is now."

"That could be anybody."

"Just keep him away from me, that's all."

Christopher saw the soap opera surgeon, too. Typically, the man played to the crowd, making faces and waving.

"Isn't he just too good-looking," someone said.

Christopher gritted his teeth. He saw the surgeon as competition, not for air time, but for Susan Arthur. The surgeon was one of her make-believe lovers. For his part, Christopher wanted something more real.

With that in mind, he said to hell with the cloudburst and left the shelter. But he didn't get far before a squad of Gestapo, all marching in step, rounded a corner and descended upon him as if he were an Allied spy. They were a contingent from "Battleguard," ABN's prime-time exploitation of World War II.

He tried to surrender, but they were taking no prisoners. They bayonetted his raincoat.

Muttering at the absurdity of mixing local and network television, Christopher fled. But instead of heading for reality, he sprinted toward the nearest soundstage.

He flung himself on the operating table and begged the beautiful doctor to save his life. Such a request was commonplace for Dr. Janice Owen, staff surgeon at "Emergency Hospital." She called for anaesthetic and a scalpel.

"Only a kiss can save me," Christopher said. "That and dinner with you tonight."

The doctor, who'd been passed from intern to male nurse as the plot of the soap opera called for, said primly, "I don't kiss on first dates."

"I'm dead then."

With a provocative smile, she licked her camera-lush lips. She was a blond, blue-eyed sex symbol to everyone addicted to afternoon television.

"This would be our second date, if you count the interview," he said.

A week ago, Christopher had interviewed the good doctor, really actress Susan Arthur, as part of his series of reports on soap operas, concentrating, of course, on those produced by his own network. Normally, such self-puffery would have caused him to rebel, but meeting Susan had silenced his scruples. His reports had yet to air, which gave him some leverage. But pride wouldn't allow him to blackmail the actress for a date.

"Scalpel!" Susan shouted.

Nurse Angela rushed over to join the fun. She peered down at the patient on the operating table and said, "Doctor, this looks like a hopeless case to me."

"That's what I've been trying to say," Christopher agreed. "Put me out of my misery."

Angela handed the doctor a scalpel. The blade gleamed under the klieg lights.

"We ought to cut out his heart," Nurse Angela said.

"Reporters don't have them," Christopher replied.

"About that date," Susan said, fingering the edge of the blade. "Just how badly do you want to go out with me?"

Angela took a step back. "I didn't know this was personal." With that she turned and walked away.

"I think you may have an admirer there," Susan taunted.

Christopher eyed the retreating woman skeptically. By comparison to Susan, Nurse Angela was plain.

"She probably admires my work."

"Some newsman you are." Susan jabbed the dull scalpel into Christopher's ample stomach, reminding him that he ought to lose twenty pounds at least.

"Is this a rehearsal?" an ancient prop man interrupted.

"It's the real thing," Christopher answered.

"What's that mean?" the man asked. His partner, young by union standards, not yet sixty by the looks of him, couldn't take his eyes off Susan's breasts, which were pushing her white hospital coat to its limits.

"We're not rehearsing," Susan said.

"Speak for yourself," Christopher added.

"We're moving this table then," said the old prop man. "We've got to make a quick set change."

In the language of the props union, that meant working at a snail's pace.

"We don't give free rides," the young one said.

Christopher hopped off the table. Even the younger man, Christopher noticed, shuffled along as though he were a senior citizen.

"I've got to change for my next scene anyway," Susan announced and started to leave.

Tagging along, Christopher asked, "What about my date?"

Her answer was interrupted by the beeping of his electronic page.

Christopher switched to transmit, acknowledging the summons. Then he switched back to receive and turned up the volume.

The voice of Wayne Gossett, Channel 3's assignment editor, echoed on the soundstage. "Outside Stage C, Christopher. An accident. One dead already. More on the way."

4

TEN YEARS IN the news business hadn't hardened Christopher to the sight of blood. But he did manage to keep from being sick, something the doctors and nurses from "Emergency Hospital" couldn't say for themselves. The sight of what real medical teams had to go through turned several stomachs and forced studio security guards to form a human barricade against such messy intrusions.

Christopher had been only yards away from the scene when his beeper had sounded. Even so, two bodies were already covered with plastic tarps by the time he arrived. The injured, half a dozen of them, had been moved undercover of Stage C's overhanging roof. The sounds coming from the Gestapo men, one high-pitched scream in particular, set off sympathetic vibrations in Christopher's stomach. He swallowed repeatedly. Only the sight of F-Stop and Scanlon pushing through the hard-nosed Los Angeles police calmed the reporter, who realized that the LAPD had suddenly taken over from studio security.

He told his rebellious stomach there was work to do and joined his crew. F-Stop immediately positioned the Ikegami electronic camera on his shoulder, while Scanlon pulled his earphones into place. Both men were soaked, as was Christopher, who'd rushed from the soundstage without his raincoat.

"What have you got so far?" the reporter asked.

"Only you," his cameraman answered.

With a grunt, Christopher clipped his press pass onto the breast pocket of his jacket, took the microphone Scanlon offered, and homed in on a paramedic whose patient, a Gestapo corporal, looked more frightened than hurt. A bystander was trying to shelter the injured man with an umbrella. But the wind-driven rain wasn't cooperating.

"A broken leg," the paramedic volunteered.

"What about the others?"

"Two dead, counting the old woman. Two more in bad shape. One doubtful."

The microphone moved to the soldier with the broken leg, whose eyes were set in shock. He began to speak without being questioned. "It wasn't an accident. He did it on purpose."

"A hit-and-run," the paramedic put in.

"Why would he do it?" the Gestapo man asked.

"He?" Christopher prompted.

"A doctor. Like him." The man was pointing at one of the onlookers from "Emergency Hospital." "I saw his green operating clothes."

The paramedic called over a stretcher and prepared to move the injured "corporal." After F-Stop got a shot of the man being loaded into a waiting ambulance, Christopher led his crew in search of another eyewitness.

A lighting technician volunteered. "I was on my way to the coffee machine and saw it all. It was murder. No doubt about it. The guy did it deliberately."

"What guy?"

"I couldn't see his face. He was wearing one of those surgical masks. But it was someone from 'Emergency Hospital.' I'm sure of it."

Christopher searched the growing crowd, immediately spotting Lieutenant Mike Baker, LAPD's press officer, who worked out of Parker Center downtown.

"Who's in charge?" Christopher shouted at him.

The cop trotted over. "Until the detectives arrive, I am."

"You'd better listen to this guy then. His story matches what I heard from one of the victims."

The camera kept rolling.

As soon as Baker heard the lighting man's statement, the lieutenant ordered his men to hold everyone from "Emergency Hospital."

28

"As a precaution only," Baker explained into the reporter's microphone.

Once the "Emergency Hospital" roundup began, protest came immediately from Channel 3's sales manager, Edgar Flemming, who was himself a witness. The man, usually so immaculate, looked a mess. Without a raincoat, his expensive suit had gotten soaked; his trousers were plastered against his legs. He was shivering from cold and the lack of a coat to keep the wind out. But that didn't stop him from going after Lieutenant Baker. "You've got no right to arrest these people," the sales manager said through clenched teeth. "They've got a show to get out."

"No one's being arrested," the policeman soothed. "We just want to ask some questions."

"I'm alerting the legal department right now," Flemming said and sent someone to phone. When he realized that Christopher's crew was videotaping his every move, the executive gestured angrily. "Forget it. I'm not going on the news."

The reporter gave his cameraman a phony cut sign, standard for occasions like this, when a witness turned reluctant. With luck, Flemming would change his mind before news time. Christopher dropped the microphone to his side, where it wasn't so obvious but would still pick up the salesman's every word.

"We need a live interview for 'The Six O'Clock News,'" the reporter said.

"Find someone else."

"We're starting Sweeps."

With a curse, Flemming rubbed a shaking hand over his wet face.

"What happened exactly?" Christopher asked.

The executive took several deep breaths before replying. "I just happened to be walking by when the ambulance plowed into the crowd." He shuddered. "One of the bodies—the old lady—just missed me."

"We need your interview."

Flemming went on as if he hadn't heard. "She flew right

29

through the air. If I hadn't ducked . . ." He grimaced at the memory.

"What were you doing out here without a raincoat?"

"I had an umbrella." The sales manager looked around as if searching for it. Then he shrugged and added, "I definitely won't go on the air. You'll have to get someone else."

Christopher was already looking for a replacement. Other than Flemming, the best bet seemed to be either the lighting technician or Mike Baker. Of course, it was the lieutenant's job to make such statements. And like most cops, he was a deadly bore on camera.

"I knew her, you know," Flemming added. "Not to speak to, but I've seen her around the lot for years."

Christopher stiffened. Bile started up his throat. He swallowed it down. "Who was she?" His voice had suddenly lost its on-air timbre.

"A cleaning woman. I don't know her name."

Without another word, Christopher turned his back on the Channel 3 executive, tossed the mike to Scanlon, then hurried over to where Lieutenant Baker was supervising the loading of the last of the wounded into an ambulance. As soon as the vehicle pulled away, the reporter said, "I want to look at the bodies."

"Not until the coroner arrives. Besides, since when did you start showing stiffs on the news?"

"I may know one of them. Personally."

The cop peered into Christopher's stricken face and shrugged. "All right, Bob. But you owe me one. Who do you want to see, the woman or the man?"

"The woman."

Baker ordered the tarp removed. The two uniformed cops who were standing guard exchanged grim looks, then patted the plastic to make certain they had the right item.

Rain water, which had accumulated in the folds of the material, ran onto Irma O'Donnell's face as soon as they exposed her. The run-off cleansed away some of the blood.

A tremor wobbled Christopher's legs. He knelt too

quickly, one knee thudding painfully against the asphalt. When he started to reach out to Irma, Baker warned, "Don't touch."

Guilt added to the reporter's already queasy stomach. Irma had said she was afraid for her life, and now she was dead. He should have taken her seriously. Yet even if he had, what could he have done? Nothing, reason told him. But conscience overrode reason.

"The witnesses are right," Christopher said. "This was murder."

Quickly, he outlined what Irma had told him the night before.

Baker, possibly a good cop before he'd given up the street for public relations, told Christopher he was crazy, adding, "Who'd want to kill someone like her? A mugger? Perhaps. But not a maniac in the middle of a television studio."

"She must have been telling the truth."

"The truth as she believed it, maybe."

"I believe it. What about the money somebody was giving her?"

Baker cocked his head skeptically. "It will certainly make a great story on the news."

"Is that what you think I'm after?"

"What I believe isn't important. The detectives are here. Tell them your story."

Christopher did just that. They weren't openly skeptical; they took careful notes once they'd ushered him out of the weather and into Stage C. That was where Herb Reisner found them.

The news director exploded at the sight of Christopher sitting down, drinking coffee. "The producers are going crazy. You've got the lead story on the 'Six O'Clock.' Our own exclusive."

"I sent F-Stop back with the tape."

"We're going live from the scene." Reisner checked his watch. "That gives you less than an hour to get your script ready."

It was later than Christopher had thought. "I had some important information to give the police."

The two detectives who'd been questioning him said nothing.

"Two can play that game," Reisner said. "With what I know, I'll be your live interview."

"Flemming was the best eyewitness."

"Flemming went home."

Christopher shook his head. A sales manager lived and died by the ratings. And here they were on the first day of Sweeps Week, the ultimate rating period, with a chance to grab good numbers with an exclusive. So it didn't make sense for a man like Flemming to just walk away.

"I don't understand it," the reporter said. "That man hasn't stopped selling since he was hustling used cars."

Reisner nodded smugly at the detectives. "I've got a better story." He paused, apparently waiting for a response. When none came he made a face and said, "The AWL called and took credit for what happened here."

"The AWL?" Christopher asked.

"The Anti-War League, they called themselves. Said they were tired of the networks pandering to war-lovers. Apparently they hate 'Battleguard' in particular. Except for the old lady, all the victims were actors in that show. For that matter, they were Gestapo." He nodded as if his comment explained everything.

"I've never heard of the AWL," the reporter said.

"What time did they call?" one of the detectives asked.

The news director closed one eye. "Right after the accident, the phones in the newsroom went crazy. Everyone pitched in, me included. Lucky I did, because I was the one who took their call. It couldn't have been more than a few minutes after the fact. So I figure they have to be involved. Otherwise, how would they know about it so quickly?"

For the first time, the detectives showed some enthusiasm. And Christopher couldn't blame them. Certainly the AWL was a better lead than an old woman obsessed by St. Christopher.

"Do you have everything you need from my reporter?" Reisner asked the policemen.

Their "yesses" came so quickly that Christopher knew it was now up to him to pursue Irma's story. If he didn't, she'd haunt him forever.

"Come on, St. Christopher," the news director said sweetly, "you've got work to do."

The reporter allowed himself to be led away. Once in the newsroom, he changed into dry clothes, kept on hand for just such emergencies. For the next half hour, he screened videotape and worked on his script. Even so, Irma was never out of his mind.

And when he joined his camera crew for their live report at the top of "The Six O'Clock News," her blood on the wall outside Stage C served as a reminder that he had let her down. He shivered inside his heavy-duty rain gear.

Throughout the live interview with Reisner, who made the AWL sound like hardcore terrorists on the order of the PLO, Christopher kept seeing Irma's face as she asked him for help. When the news insert was over, the reporter slumped against the stucco wall of Stage C. He didn't have the heart to think about "The Eleven O'Clock News" still ahead of him.

"You were rotten," the news director complained, shielding his lapel mike in his fist as a precaution against technical error, or a disgruntled audio man. "Get some life into it for the 'Eleven.' Write a new script. Do something."

"I'm following up on the old woman."

"Don't get personally involved," Reisner said.

"That's the way I work."

The news director pulled off his microphone and handed it to Scanlon, who immediately fled the rain by ducking inside Stage C. "From what you told me, she sounds like she had a screw loose."

"I need your help, Herb. I want to concentrate full time on this. That will mean freeing me from all other assignments."

Rolling his eyes, the news director made a show of his exasperation.

"If I'm right," Christopher went on, "Channel 3 will get credit for solving a murder."

"That will be the day," Reisner replied, moving to join the reporter against the stucco wall. There, at least, the rain could only get at their feet. "I hate to say this, Bob, but you're important to our news. I can't take you off regular assignments during Sweeps."

"This is something I have to do."

"On your own time, Bob."

Christopher took a deep breath. "I'm going over your head on this, Herb."

"I make a bad enemy."

"I'm sorry," the reporter said.

"Oh, hell. At least you told me to my face. Do what you want as long as I don't have to take responsibility for gambling with our ratings."

Christopher approached the executive bungalow with some misgiving. Normally, he would never have imposed on his friendship with Wyn Brewster, Channel 3's station manager. But Irma was not to be denied.

The bungalow itself, completely Californian with white stucco walls and a red tile roof, stood near the front gate. The building dated back to the silent-movie era, as did the entire studio lot. Over the years, the bungalow had been remodeled constantly, but only on the inside. The exterior had been designated as an historical landmark long ago, and had a brass plaque to prove it.

Wyn Brewster's secretary, Norma Lewis, was a landmark too. She had survived countless administrations in a business where longevity was counted in weeks, not years.

"What's your secret?" Christopher had asked her once.

Instead of answering, Norma had smiled enigmatically. Now she disappeared through the door on which hung a fourteen-carat nameplate: WYN T. BREWSTER, a memento dating back to his days as sales manager.

Norma returned a moment later to usher Christopher inside. At first glance, Brewster looked small because of the enormous office. But he was nearly six feet tall, a man who flaunted baldness by cropping what hair remained close against his skull. He wore a perpetual smile, the mark of a good salesman, he claimed. Although Brewster claimed to be a man who worshiped the future, he collected the past. Walnut book shelves covering two walls were crammed with collectibles: Quaker Oats boxes from the Thirties, Moxie Cola signs, punch boards that offered long-forgotten prizes, even a Mobil flying horse that lit up. Amid the memorabilia four nineteen-inch TV sets were sandwiched to monitor all the network stations in town.

Christopher dripped on the huge oriental rug that overlaid the wall-to-wall carpeting.

Brewster slapped the reporter on the shoulder, grinned, and said, "Are you in trouble again?"

"What makes you say that?"

"I know that look of yours."

On more than one occasion Brewster had interceded on Christopher's behalf, particularly when Governor Dale Cody had tried to pressure ABN executives to have the reporter fired. The governor claimed that Christopher was biased, and had been since the days when Cody owned Channel 3. That was before his election, after which the governor had to divest himself of such interests.

Just how Brewster managed to prevail against so formidable an enemy Christopher never knew. For that matter, the reporter didn't quite understand how he and Brewster got to be such good friends. Of course they had both started working at Channel 3 on the same day five years before, sharing the indignities of indoctrination heaped upon them by the personnel department.

"Did you see the 'Six O'Clock'?" Christopher asked.

"A hell of a story, even if it did land right in our lap."

"The woman who died, Irma O'Donnell, she came to me for help last night."

"Is this going to be another of your crusades?"

"She was afraid of being killed."

"She told you that?"

Christopher nodded.

"What else?"

"Nothing specific. That's why it's up to me to find out what really happened."

"And the police?"

"I don't think they believe me."

"Why?" Brewster wanted to know.

"They figure she just got in the way, that the Gestapo was the real target."

"Did they say that?"

"I could read it in their faces," Christopher said.

Brewster picked up a Quaker Oats box and shook it. Antique cereal rattled inside. "Just what are you asking from me, Bob?"

"To be released from all other duties so I can follow up on this."

The station manager dropped the Quaker Oats container. Stooping, he retrieved and reshelved the relic before replying. "I know how you must feel, Bob. I really do. But you've got to understand what local news ratings mean to a station manager. So goes the news, so goes my career. Hellsakes, you're content right here. You're having a ball with your crusades. But me, I've got my sights set on a network slot in New York. You know how much that means to me."

"You've never made any secret of it."

"It's something I have to do."

"I feel the same about the old woman."

The station manager paced back and forth across the Oriental rug. Once he stopped to switch his Mobil horse on and off. "What does Reisner say?"

"He knows I came here."

"That means he wants you to stay on the news."

"He'll survive without me."

"But will I?" Brewster took a tissue from his desk and dusted one of his Moxie Cola signs. He actually kept a six-pack of the stuff around somewhere, occasionally offering to open one of the forty-year-old bottles for anyone who had the guts to drink it. So far there'd been no takers.

"If I come up with a story," Christopher said, "Channel 3 will look pretty damn good."

"We're in sweeps, Bob. You solve a murder this week and fine, we're in clover as far as the ratings go. But can you promise to deliver results on schedule?" Brewster shook his head. "I know the answer to that as well as you do. Even Sherlock Holmes couldn't make such a guarantee."

"I can't let it drop."

The station manager swore. "I don't know how Reisner puts up with you."

"He needs me."

"And so do I."

"I'm asking for a favor," Christopher said.

"I've never made any claims on you before, Bob. But you owe me."

"I know that."

"Then you've got to understand why I'm turning you down. I need those ratings. Hell, I'm not getting any younger. This may be my last chance at New York."

Christopher stared at his friend. Brewster was thirty-three, two years younger than the reporter. But in New York, it wasn't uncommon for network vice-presidents to burn out before they reached thirty.

Christopher asked for a drink.

The station manager slid back a panel behind his desk to reveal a wet bar. Without asking, Brewster popped the top on a can of diet soda and handed it to Christopher with the comment, "We've got to watch that weight of yours."

37

"Don't change the subject."

"All right, Bob. I know you. You won't let go of a thing like this. But I can be just as stubborn. Still, I'll compromise this time. Promise me one consumer report a day and I'll let you off the hook on anything else."

Christopher's normal output, when there was no storm emergency, was one such report a day. To produce even that much was a full-time job. He knew that and so did Brewster. So there really wasn't much of a compromise as far as the station manager was concerned. But what he didn't know was that Christopher had half a dozen reports squirreled away for just such an emergency. Of course, he'd have to go live to update them each night, but that wouldn't tie him up for more than a couple of hours.

"Okay, it's a deal," he said, but immediately felt guilty for tricking his friend. He might have confessed the sin if Brewster hadn't joked about his waistline.

That brought more guilt, reminding the reporter that he was within one belt notch of disaster. A few more pounds and he'd have to buy a new wardrobe, not to mention the fines he'd have to pay for going over Reisner's weight limit. "Anything beyond that," the news director liked to say, "and you'll remind our viewers of their own intemperance."

Brewster came around his desk to clap a hand on Christopher's shoulder. "I want you to keep me informed, Bob. You can fill me in tomorrow at the usual time."

Lunch in the studio commissary was a weekly ritual of theirs.

"There's a new diet I want you to try. I've had it put on the menu especially for you." He poked Christopher's stomach. "Whatever you're on now sure as hell doesn't seem to be working."

"The studio diet," Christopher reminded him. "That was your idea too."

"Oh, yeah. All greens, right?"

The reporter nodded.

"That sounds like a crackpot idea to me."

Christopher agreed by sticking his tongue out.

"Don't eat anything yellow," Brewster advised. "Otherwise you'll turn blue." With that, the station manager escorted Christopher to the door.

As they were about to part, Brewster said, "One more thing. Keep a low profile on this Irma O'Donnell thing. A story like today's is good for ratings. But we wouldn't want people to get the idea that Channel 3 is a hotbed of maniacs. So no bad publicity, huh? Not now, not when we've got a chance to be the number one station in this town. And you know what that means." The station manager clicked his heels together. "If Channel 3 is number one, so am I."

As the reporter left the office, he could hear Brewster singing, "I love New York."

5

AT FIRST GLANCE, Christopher thought a wildcat strike had closed down Stage C. Then he realized that the two prop men just inside the sliding doors actually were moving, pretending to struggle with a cardboard wall, an "Emergency Hospital" backdrop that couldn't have weighed more than a few pounds.

"Did either of you two see the accident?" the reporter asked, beginning his quest for new information.

"When do we have time to see anything?" one of them complained. "They work us to death around here."

His aged companion agreed with a wobbly nod of his head. "That hit-and-run raised hell with our schedule. We're on late call right now." He rubbed gnarled hands together eagerly. "Of course that means overtime."

"They don't show us any consideration," the other said. "We didn't volunteer."

But their seamed smiles said they loved the time-and-a-half just the same.

"Did you see anything at all?" Christopher persisted.

"Hold it!" bellowed a male voice.

Startled, Christopher turned to see Kraut Wagner, shop steward for props, charging across the sound stage. "You want to talk to my boys, see me first."

The reporter gestured surrender to union jurisdiction before repeating his question.

"My boys don't have time to wander around the lot sightseeing," Kraut replied.

"Besides," his eldest put in, "it's raining out there."

Kraut glared. "Get that wall stowed away. We're shooting a new scene in a few minutes. It may even have a little sex in it. You wouldn't want to miss that."

The wall, on dollies, squeaked away.

"I'll talk to you later," Christopher called after the two oldtimers.

"If there really is any sex," the shop steward said, "they won't have the energy."

Kraut, a man in his fifties who'd come to props after twenty years in the army as a supply sergeant, poked himself in the chest with a tobacco-stained thumb and said, "Just remember. I do the talking for my boys."

On good days, the shop steward dressed as though poverty-stricken. Today, he was wearing olive-drab fatigues that still had his name printed over the breast pocket. His combat boots squeaked worse than the dolly wheels.

"I know you, Christopher. I don't want any trouble."

"I'm not after you or your boys."

Kraut shrugged, then tugged at his fatigue pants, which refused to climb beyond his protruding stomach.

"Think about it this way, Kraut. It could have been one of your boys out there in those body bags."

The shop steward scratched his belly. "We were taping a scene when it happened. So nobody around here could have seen anything. I told that to the cops already."

"Witnesses outside say the guy driving the ambulance was from your show."

"So the cops told me. But anybody can get hold of a surgical outfit. We use the real things, you know. We get the stuff from a medical supply house."

"Where do you keep them?"

"I do all the ordering. After they're used, they go to wardrobe for cleaning and pressing. It's wardrobe's responsibility to keep them hanging in the dressing rooms."

"What about the ambulance, then? That's your prop, isn't it?"

Kraut nodded, running a hand over his sparse hair, still cut to military whitewalls around the ears. "I keep it tuned up and gassed, if that's what you mean."

"Who keeps the keys?"

"I do," the steward admitted. "In the property box here on stage. But I lock it up when I'm not around."

"Are the keys missing?"

"They were right where they should be when the police checked."

Christopher already knew that the ambulance had been discovered abandoned behind the scenic warehouse. No keys had been found in the ignition.

"What about extra sets?"

"Two pairs of keys came with the car. One's lost. But that's par for the course around here. Hell, actors will steal you blind if you let 'em."

"I know you drive the ambulance for your own personal use," Christopher said, not knowing that at all, but figuring Kraut to take all the perks that came his way.

"So?"

"Did you tell the police that?"

"What they say about you is true," the shop steward grumbled. "You *are* a bastard."

"Only when I have to be."

"Just what do you want from me?"

Christopher paused to think that over. As shop steward, Kraut had very few duties, certainly nothing that would keep him from seeing everything that happened on or around Stage C. It was just a question of whether the man had been napping at the wrong time.

"Did you spot anything unusual today?" the reporter asked.

"What do you mean by unusual?"

"Don't play dumb with me, Kraut."

The shop steward laughed. "I learned that trick my first week in the army. Play dumb long enough and you can usually get someone else to do your job for you."

Christopher clenched his teeth.

"All right," Kraut said. "But you aren't going to like it." He leaned close as if to savor the reporter's reaction. "I saw someone sitting in the ambulance during a break earlier today. That someone was your lady friend Susan

Arthur. So it stands to reason she could have taken the keys easily enough."

Christopher was about to demand further explanation when the warning buzzer sounded on stage. Taping was about to begin.

Lights came up on a nursing station backdrop in the intensive care unit. This was the domain of Nurse Angela, at the moment in heated argument with Dr. Janice Owen.

"I can't leave my post," the nurse protested.

"I'll be right here," the doctor answered.

Even to Christopher, who didn't follow the soap, it was obvious that the doctor wanted Nurse Angela out of the way for some ulterior motive.

"There are rules to be followed," Angela insisted.

"How would you like a transfer to the night shift?"

"There's nothing you can do to me that hasn't been done already."

As the scene unfolded, Christopher agonized. Gazing at his beautiful Susan, he couldn't imagine what she'd been doing in the ambulance. She was a staff doctor, after all, not a paramedic.

His anxious sigh brought a warning glance from the stage manager. Embarrassed, the reporter grinned self-consciously.

Susan spoke in her doctor's voice, "You're relieved of duty, Nurse Evans."

"We'll see about that," Angela responded sharply. She stalked noisily down a backdrop corridor.

Janice Owen immediately picked up the phone at the nurse's station and dialed an internal number. Then, in a sex-laden voice, she whispered, "She's gone, darling. Meet me here."

Susan's face, now in closeup, had taken on that special glow she reserved for the men in her soap-opera life.

"Hurry," she said and hung up. Impatiently, she sorted through a stack of files. Every so often she looked off-camera expectantly. Finally she began to fidget.

Dr. Peter Moore, the surgeon who had gotten away

with murder at "Emergency Hospital," had missed his cue.

"Cut!" yelled the stage manager. "Where's Mark?"

Mark Lambert was the actor portraying the murderous medic.

Screams of outrage boomed over the loudspeaker. "We're on overtime," the director railed. "Find that lazy bastard."

"We're in the money tonight," Kraut rhapsodized at Christopher's shoulder. "Once mistakes start happening, there's no end to them."

The reporter turned to stare at the shop steward for a moment. When he looked back at the intensive care unit, the cast had disappeared, along with stage manager and cameramen. Only Kraut and his boys remained behind.

"Haste makes waste," Kraut reminded his prop crew. "Let's not work ourselves out of a job."

At his words, the men slowed to a stunted dance choreographed by union ritual.

"Where's Susan?" Christopher asked the shop steward.

Kraut broke pace with his peers to shrug in real time. "Probably looking for Lambert like everyone else."

"Does he disappear often?"

"Only when he's snorting a little extra."

Christopher found himself wondering if he, too, ought to join the search. But for his own peace of mind, he decided to keep after the shop steward who, the reporter now felt certain, was holding back vital information. With a man like Kraut, however, it was impossible to tell if he had something to hide or was merely being uncooperative.

"How did you happen to see Susan in the ambulance?"

The shop steward's face puckered into what the reporter took to be a smirk. "Watching beautiful women is a hobby of mine."

Christopher knew that to be a lie. If Kraut watched anything it was beautiful men.

"Was Mark Lambert with her?" the reporter asked.

"What makes you say that?"

"Just a guess." But a good one, since the actor was the most beautiful man on "Emergency Hospital."

"I could get to dislike you, Christopher."

"Would money help?"

Kraut licked his lips. "I don't take checks."

The reporter opened his wallet. He had two twenties, one of which he promptly offered.

The bill was added to a wad that already produced an obscene bulge in Kraut's fatigue pocket.

"She was sitting in the ambulance with Lambert, all right. Not that I care where he sits."

"What were they doing?"

"I didn't let them out of my sight, I can tell you. So I can say with absolute certainty that all they did was talk. But I kept my eye on them just the same, because you know what talk can lead to. Even when the other guy arrived, I kept watch."

Kraut paused and shook his head as if regretting what he'd just said. "I mean that ambulance was coming up in another scene, so it was my duty to keep an eye on it. You can't blame a man in my position for looking out for his own interests."

"Who was the other man?"

"Ed Flemming, though why he was on the set of a network show I don't know. He's strictly local sales. But then Susan attracts them all, as you ought to know."

"What were they talking about?"

"How should I know? They closed themselves in that damned ambulance. But they were pretty friendly in there, I can tell you. After a while, the windows got so steamed up I couldn't see what the hell was going on." The shop steward looked pained.

"And that's it? They just sat in the ambulance and talked?"

"That old crate wasn't rocking on its springs, if that's what you mean." Kraut scratched at one of his whitewalls.

45

"All I can figure is your Susan must have been checking out a scene. Though the director ought to have been there for that. They got a union, too, you know."

"I don't understand."

"You're not listening, Christopher. After Mark and the salesman left, she climbed in the back of the ambulance by herself and lay down. Hell, it's not all that comfortable in there. And I ought to know. I've tried it often enough. On my breaks, you understand."

More than anything, Christopher wanted to grab the man and shake him. But the reporter restrained himself. All he did was nod encouragement.

"The way I figure it," Kraut continued, "the script must call for Susan to become a patient in her own hospital."

"Don't you know for sure?"

"I never read that crap. But I can tell you one thing. The way she was lying in there on her back, with her hands folded on her chest, it reminded me of a hearse, not an ambulance."

6

A SCREAM, MORE chilling than any ever before produced on the set of "Emergency Hospital," tore at Christopher's ears. He careened into a maternity ward backdrop. A real wheelchair barked his shins. But that didn't stop him from charging toward the sound, toward Susan's dressing room.

But he didn't get that far. He found the actress peering inside Mark Lambert's open door. She was about to let go with another scream when Christopher grabbed her.

Mark Lambert sat staring at himself in a light-circled mirror. What appeared to fascinate the actor's dead eyes was the scalpel protruding from his chest. Seeing the weapon, Christopher had the unsettling sensation that it might be the same blade Susan had playfully threatened to use on him earlier.

A cast intern arrived on the scene out of breath, took one look, and wobbled against the corridor wall. An "Emergency Hospital" nurse grabbed hold of her giddy colleague as she skidded in the blood puddled on the linoleum. Only the two propmen arriving at a breakneck walk looked unaffected.

"Call the police," Christopher told the pair. To the others he said, "Stay out of Lambert's dressing room until they get here."

Then, hugging Susan's trembling form to him, the reporter led her down the hall to her own dressing room, where he used the phone to call the assignment desk. Wayne Gossett was still there, high on overtime and adrenaline.

Quickly, Christopher reported the situation.

An obscene whoop shrilled over the line.

"One more thing," Christopher added. "There's a sur-

47

gical gown hanging on the back of the dead man's door. The gown's still damp enough to have been out in the rain yesterday."

"Another exclusive," the assignment editor yelped, "and I haven't got a crew within twenty miles."

"Get me F-Stop."

"I don't want him working late. He's already had his fair share of overtime."

"He knows the story. I won't have to waste my breath briefing him."

"What's to brief?" Gossett countered. "All you've got to do is tape the stiff. Tastefully of course. Any cameraman can do that."

"You're wasting time, Wayne."

Time was the magic word with Gossett. His very existence depended on split-second timing as he met one deadline after another throughout the day.

"All right, you win. Consider it done." He hung up.

Christopher turned back to Susan, expecting to find her craving comfort. But she no longer needed a shoulder to lean on; she had a joint going.

"I've never seen a dead man up close before," she said dreamily, then offered the marijuana cigarette to Christopher.

He declined with a tic-like shake of his head.

Susan shrugged and went back to inhaling deeply. A moment later she wondered, "Why would he do it?"

"Do what?"

"Mark must have driven the ambulance. The wet gown proves that."

Surprised that she'd noticed the garment, Christopher opened his mouth to question her about it. But then he decided that could wait. Right now, he had a job to do, because it wasn't often a reporter got this kind of jump on the police.

"Susan, I hate to leave you alone," he began, then saw that she had already left him for a dream world of her own. He kissed her on the forehead before slipping out the door.

Lambert's dressing room was a replica of Susan's, with just enough space for a small makeup table and two worn-out chairs, one of which the dead man occupied. On the other sat a portable videotape recorder, loaded and ready for playback. The hand-lettered label on the cassette was easy enough to read across the cramped room: "Getting the Kinks Out."

Bingo Bradford's work, unless Christopher missed his guess. But getting to the machine and proving Bingo's omnipresence was easier said than done. Blood had spilled over much of the linoleum and leaving footprints didn't seem like a good idea.

Christopher squirmed, itching to get at the tape. In his eagerness, his shoulder brushed against the dressing room door, partially dislodging Lambert's nameplate. The impermanent placard had been taped in place, a reminder from network management that soap stars were expendable.

The reporter was about to leap for a dry spot of floor when a hand restrained him. It belonged to a woman who had a police badge clipped to the lapel of her large, stylishly cut jacket.

Flustered, Christopher opened his mouth to explain his intentions. But the cop spoke first. "I recognize you from the news." Her tone was neutral enough, but her grim expression condemned all TV journalists. "I'm Detective Duffy and this is my partner, Sergeant Nelson."

Both officers were the same height, slightly under six feet. But Duffy had fifty pounds on her emaciated partner, and none of it fat. Nelson's intensity, however, made up for his lack of bulk. Of the two, Christopher couldn't tell who might be the most dangerous. He sighed and waited for the inevitable onslaught. Cops loved nothing better than to intimidate newsmen.

But they ignored him to study the body from the doorway. After a while they announced that crossing the threshhold would be left to experts from the coroner's office. Until then, the dressing room was strictly off-limits.

With that taken care of, the two detectives led Christopher back to the stage area, where they began questioning both cast and crew. During all that time, the reporter's camera crew was kept waiting outside. The thought of it had him fuming and pacing. He knew damn well that the scene of another murder, a second Channel 3 exclusive by virtue of location, would call for live cut-ins throughout the evening to hype "The Eleven O'Clock News." Especially during Sweeps. Yet all the onstage TV monitors showed were occasional bulletin slides. If Herb Reisner was running true to form, he'd be screaming for blood by now. Christopher's blood.

Bent on pleading such a life-and-death situation, the reporter accosted the detectives while they were trying to make sense out of Jason, in reality actor Ted Holland, one of "Emergency Hospital's" longstanding characters. Each time that it looked as though his role was about to disappear from the soap, a plot twist would resurrect it. He'd begun as a homosexual before marrying Nurse Angela. At the moment, Jason was awaiting final approval for his sex-change operation. In the interim, he was receiving hormone shots. To play such a role, Holland wore heavy, feminine makeup, and did his best to stay in character whenever he was on the set, whether cameras were rolling or not.

He kissed Christopher on the cheek.

The reporter squirmed, but continued to demand his rights from the detectives.

Gingerly, Nelson said, "You can't expect the privileges of a newsman when you're a participant."

"Is that a polite way of calling me a suspect?"

"Aren't we all, darling?" Holland asked, grabbing Christopher and biting him on the neck.

"Ugh," the reporter spat out, shoving the actor away and into the arms of the arriving Herb Reisner.

One look at the news director's livid face and the actor said, "I'm in love."

Reisner responded with a roar. "What the hell's going on? I've got a camera crew waiting outside in the rain at time-and-a-half."

"*We* don't get overtime," Nelson complained. "Not in cash anyway."

"This is a big story," Reisner half shouted while managing to keep Jason-Holland at arm's length. "I want my crew in here."

"Unrequited," Holland breathed and minced from the stage.

Duffy watched the exit carefully before saying, "You know the rules. No cameras allowed until our crews have gone over the crime scene."

According to Reisner the only rules worth worrying about were his own.

"I want one of you to do a live interview for the news," Reisner informed the detectives, a demand, not a request. "The public has a right to know about murder."

"Who said anything about murder?" Duffy asked.

The news director glared at Christopher. "That's the report our assignment desk got."

"It could be suicide," the female detective added.

"With a scalpel in the chest?" Christopher interjected.

"There's no telling what loonies will do," Nelson answered for her. "Maybe he got to thinking he was a real doctor."

"Knowing Christopher," Reisner said, "he probably thinks this is part of a conspiracy, beginning with the old lady."

The detectives exchanged quick glances. "What old lady?" they asked in unison.

And so once again the reporter replayed his midnight conversation with Irma O'Donnell. To which Duffy's only answer was a sigh, while Nelson settled for a scowl of disbelief.

"What about my murder?" Reisner persisted.

51

"You tell him," Nelson said wearily to his partner.

Duffy pursed her lips momentarily. "There's a good chance Lambert went nuts, though don't quote us. Hell, watching the soaps could turn any brain to mush. So God only knows what acting in the things might do to you. Anyway, the ambulance bit could have been an accident to start with, but then Lambert's conscience got the better of him. Maybe he was drunk or on drugs when he drove the damn thing. So it's more likely suicide than murder."

Christopher snorted. "Then why would he wear a surgical mask to disguise himself?"

"We don't have all the answers yet."

"And doesn't it seem strange that a woman would be killed in an accident the day after telling me her life was in danger?"

"We'll look into it."

"I don't intend to drop this," Christopher said, his voice unusually soft. "Not personally or on the news."

"Speaking of news," Reisner put in.

"Whoa, there," Nelson said. "We don't want you guys on our backs. But look at it our way. What possible connection could there be between an old cleaning woman and a well-known actor like Lambert?"

The reporter tugged his trousers up over his unruly stomach. "I don't have all the answers yet. But a little cooperation never hurt anybody."

"Just what do you have in mind?" the sergeant asked suspiciously.

"That's more like it," Reisner said, rubbing his hands together expectantly.

Christopher took a deep breath. "I want to see the videotape in Lambert's dressing room."

"What's so special about it?" the detective asked skeptically.

"If I'm not mistaken, that stuff in there is X-rated. There's been a regular epidemic around here lately."

"We're not the vice squad."

"Humor me and I'll stay off your back."

Reisner rolled his eyes. "Are you sure you know what you're doing?"

"I'm guessing about the tape," the reporter admitted. "But what else have I got?"

At that, Nelson nodded to his partner, who immediately left the stage area. While they waited for her return, the news director made faces and pointed at his watch. "The Eleven O'Clock News" was fifteen minutes away.

Christopher began to pace but he didn't get far before the female detective came back on stage to say, "They're through in the dressing room. We can play the tape."

The reporter started to move but Nelson called him back. "First," said the detective, "we want your word that you won't release any information about the tape without our permission."

As a journalist, Christopher hated strings of any kind. But he saw no option at the moment. "It's a deal," he said, cringing at the sound of his own words.

The detectives looked to Reisner for confirmation.

"Okay," the news director agreed. "Just so long as we get this over with before eleven."

Once in the dressing room, Kline nodded at the tape machine and said, "Since you're familiar with the equipment, Christopher, you do the honors."

Gingerly, the reporter wiped away the residue left behind by fingerprint men, who seemed to have gone to a lot of trouble for a suicide. Then he switched on the videotape machine. After that, he held his breath and punched the start button. The tube flared to life, flickered as if its horizontal hold was out of whack, then steadied. But there was no picture, only a snowstorm of fuzz. Whatever was on the tape originally had been completely erased.

Christopher shook his head until it ached. But his memory refused to erase. There was no ridding himself of Irma O'Donnell.

7

RESPONDING TO A Herb Reisner memo, Christopher sloshed into the newsroom an hour early the next morning. His knee-high rubber boots had failed to keep his feet dry, and his throbbing head was a reminder that old ladies and sleep didn't mix. Add to that unfulfilled fantasies of Susan and he felt as shaky as if he'd been drinking all night.

What he needed was an immediate infusion of coffee and calories. What he got was a snappy salute from Wayne Gossett, who looked disgustingly fresh and eager as he stood at attention behind his assignment desk.

"Welcome to World War Three," he announced. "Reisner has decided to do battle with the elements."

An answering grunt was the best Christopher could manage.

"He's pulled out all the stops. I can even hire a chopper."

"Nothing could fly in this stuff," the reporter muttered. "Except an assignment editor."

Raising his voice caused Christopher to grimace with pain. He had to squint to keep his head from falling off. Even so, he couldn't blot out the glare from Gossett's brightly shining plexiglass assignment board, which pinpointed crew locations and stories being covered. Multicolored grease pencils had already marked in mud slides, road closures, and a dam about to burst in La Canada.

"Any houses threatened?" the reporter asked quietly.

"Not yet, but I have high hopes."

The comment prompted another salute, after which Gossett ducked out of sight behind his desk. He reappeared a moment later wearing a steel helmet that bore civil defense symbols. It was a prop he had used before, so Christopher didn't react.

Instead, the reporter began shedding his plastic raincoat, which looked remarkably like a more expensive leather version that anchorman Al Aarons had recently purchased in a campaign of one-upmanship. Once free of the wrap, Christopher wiped his hands on a yard of discarded wire copy before staggering toward the coffee machine. He deposited a quarter in a cracked piggy bank, then couldn't find a clean cup. To wash one out meant going down the hall to the bathroom, so he settled for a dirty mug, hoping the coffee was hot enough to kill germs. It tasted like it could kill anything.

Usually, there were doughnuts that Gossett brought in. But today, the early crews assigned to cover the storm had left only crumbs behind.

"What's the meeting about?" Christopher asked, forcing himself to leave the greasy tidbits alone.

"You saw the memo. The subject is Sweeps, and, to quote our lord and master, your attendance will be greatly appreciated."

Christopher swore.

In answer the assignment editor grinned broadly. "You've got to hand it to Reisner. If he'd made the meeting mandatory, he'd have to pay overtime to all the writers and producers on the late shift. This way they have to come in on their own time."

"Maybe they won't show," Christopher said, running his tongue over his teeth to see if the coffee had left any enamel behind. But he knew, as did Gossett, that when Herb Reisner said attendance would be appreciated, the alternative was unemployment.

"Half the staff's waiting in the lunchroom already."

Christopher glanced at the clock on the wall, which was synchronized with network time. Reisner's 10:30 convocation was almost upon them.

"Pick up one of those grease pencils of yours, Wayne, and mark me down on special assignment."

Gossett answered with an obscene gesture.

"I'm serious. I'm following up on the old lady."

"Look, Bob, Sid Manning is out sick, so I'm short a reporter."

"You're short a reporter even when he's here."

"Okay. I surrender." Gossett threw up his hands. "I admit it. With this storm raising so much hell, I need you. You're the one man who never lets his on-camera ego get in the way of the story." The assignment editor's tone lost just enough of its usual malice to allow a hint of admiration to creep in. "Most of the clowns around here care more about their pretty faces than what they're reporting. While you . . . you don't seem to give a damn about how you look on camera."

"Thanks a lot."

"You know what I mean."

Strangely enough, Christopher did. The comment, coming from a man like Gossett, was a sincere compliment. Besides, Christopher recognized his own on-camera shortcomings. His nose had been broken too many times. He refused to wear color-enhancing contact lenses for his blue eyes. And his ever expanding waistline was a sign of overindulgence. But at least he looked real, or so he liked to think. At the moment, however, Irma had left him feeling anything but.

Wondering if such a battered conscience showed in a man's face, he studied himself in the mirror on the wall next to the assignment desk. The glass had been placed there so reporters could check their makeup before going on camera. God keep the viewing public from seeing a pale face or too many wrinkles.

Despite his headache, Christopher went wide-eyed at the revelation. Rain had plastered his hair so flat against his skull that it looked like a coat of black polish. And no contact lenses ever made would do anything for those bloodshot eyes, which peered from a face as pallid as a corpse.

He stuck out his tongue and nearly gagged.

Herb Reisner chose that moment to enter the newsroom at a trot, rubbing his hands together gleefully and announcing, "Is everyone ready for my big performance?" Abruptly he skidded to a stop and stared open-mouthed at his reporter. "Jesus, Bob, you look like someone from radio."

Christopher ignored the insult. He wasn't about to admit to a night of tortured dreams. So he went to his desk to type out the list he'd made during the night, a plan of attack to put Irma at rest. Heading the agenda was an interview with Channel 3 Sales Manager Edgar Flemming.

But that would have to wait for Reisner, who was about to begin his memo-announced mandatory meeting for volunteers. At 10:30 exactly, the cast assembled—editors, writers, producers, graphic artists, secretaries, production assistants, and anchormen, including sports and weather personalities, everyone who wasn't out actually covering the news. As befitted a number-one anchor constantly in search of more limelight, Al Aarons was the last to arrive. He sauntered around the room, announcing his presence with occasional nods to the favored. Nicknamed AA because of his drinking, he was a striking man—dark hair, blue eyes—with a complexion that looked made-up at all times. His baby-blues, as he liked to call them, tended to sparkle unnaturally, brightness depending on adrenaline or alcohol.

Reisner waited for his anchorman to settle into a chair. Then the news director plunged right in.

"Just so there's no doubt in any of your minds, I've called this meeting to talk about survival. In a word, that means Sweeps."

He paused for effect. AA, usually subdued this far from air time, merely nodded.

Reisner didn't miss a beat. "Let me tell you, rates rise and fall the moment that book is out. So we're talking real money here, and a lot of it. In a market the size of

57

Los Angeles, the shift of a single rating point—say from Channel 7 to us here at 3—can mean more than a million dollars in additional station revenue over the year."

Reisner stopped speaking long enough to let that sink in. When he proceeded his eyes were closed, a look of near ecstasy on his face. "A number one rating in the Sweeps book would give me bragging rights in this town."

He pointed at AA. "Think of it, Al, going on the air and saying we're number one. We've never had that privilege here at Channel 3 before."

"I always think of myself as number one," Aarons retorted, a practiced grin on his face to show that he was joking, that he was really quite humble. But nobody was fooled.

"Any questions so far?" the news director asked.

"Yeah," Gossett blurted, secure in the knowledge that few if any coveted his high-pressure, deadline-punctuated job. "What are we supposed to do about it?"

"I thought that was obvious. Get me enough good stories to destroy the competition. Houses being washed away in the flood. Kids and dogs on rafts. Dam breaks."

Reisner climbed onto the assignment desk before rhapsodizing further. "An airliner down in the storm. Even another murder. Anything to make me—us—number one."

Amid the nervous laughter that followed, Christopher was called to the phone. As soon as he identified himself, a muffled voice said, "Warmonger!"

"Pardon?"

"We will no longer tolerate the glorification of war. We will fight, kill if necessary, to put an end to it."

"The Anti-War League?" the reporter asked, realizing that until this moment he thought the AWL some kind of ratings ploy on Reisner's part.

"One of our soldiers has given his life in battle." The caller, probably a male, was holding his nose to produce a nasal disguise.

"Are you talking about Mark Lambert?"

"An actor has many roles."

Christopher didn't believe a word. Even a soap opera character wouldn't run down innocent people to protest ABN's "Battleguard." The critics were doing that already.

"What the hell do you want?" the reporter asked.

"For you to stay out of it."

If Reisner hadn't been in plain sight across the room, Christopher would have suspected the news director of making the call to get his reporter back into the Sweeps stakes.

"I'm declaring war," Christopher said, hung up, then immediately dialed a friend at the *Times*, which had a far better morgue than Channel 3. The newspaper had never heard of the AWL, which was good enough for Christopher. The calls had to be from some nut monitoring police calls.

With a sigh, Christopher rejoined the staff gathered around Reisner. But the news director had run out of things to say. All that was left were his usual closing threats.

Even after those were fully aired, Christopher still had plenty of time before his lunch meeting with Wyn Brewster. So he pulled out his checklist, donned his plastic raincoat after flapping it in Aarons's direction, and headed for the sales department.

Edgar Flemming's office gleamed so brightly Christopher had to squint. A sheet of glass balanced on highly polished chrome legs served as a desk. A longer piece of glass suspended on metallic sawhorses had been turned into a conference table, surrounded by chairs with see-through plastic seats. Fitting right in with the decor was a nine-foot couch covered in a shiny silver fabric. The material itself, rough and scratchy to the touch, was said to have left its mark on half the secretaries in the bungalow.

Flemming, a tall tanned man who sought the moneyed look of Beverly Hills, showed an assortment of labels and shook hands as if being graded on sincerity. But the grip failed to hide the gleam of dislike in his eyes, present since the day Christopher refused to mention a sponsor's product favorably in a consumer report.

"Wyn Brewster said you'd be dropping by," Flemming began, toying with a foot-high crystal paperweight in the shape of a pyramid. The ornament held down a single sheet of paper. "He asked me to cooperate." His tone gave nothing away.

Christopher saw no point in being diplomatic. Nothing would make them like one another. "I'm here to talk about your relationship with Susan Arthur."

Flemming didn't respond, merely smiled, his bright white salesman's teeth as carnivorous as ever.

"Are you having some kind of backseat romance?"

Still nothing.

"You were seen in the ambulance with her just before the hit-and-run."

The sales manager snapped his teeth. "You're jealous, aren't you?"

Not the answer Christopher had hoped for. "Tell me when you're cooperating."

Flemming spat out a toothy laugh. "Ask away."

"What about Susan?"

"You won't like the answers."

"I'll do my best to survive."

"You'd make a good salesman," Flemming said, hiding his teeth for a moment.

"I'm waiting."

"All right. You can call me Susan's procurer." He cocked his head to one side, then nodded. "Yes, I like the sound of that. It's so much nicer than pimp."

The strain of trying to remain calm brought a cramp to the back of Christopher's thigh. He needed to stretch, to knead the errant muscle. But he refused to give in to it. He refused to show weakness in front of Flemming.

"You see," the salesman went on, "I have some important clients coming in from the East, friends of the network brass in New York. I promised them Susan as a dinner partner. If things go well after that"—his tanned hands turned over and back—"well, you know what's expected."

"Not with Susan, I don't."

"There are a lot of women in television, women just as beautiful and talented as Susan. She knows that. She knows what has to be done." Flemming folded his arms across his flat stomach and looked smug.

"I don't believe you."

"Cross my heart."

"Bullshit!"

"I can sell anyone, Christopher. Even you. For instance, would you like a sample of past clients she has . . . shall we say, serviced?"

The reporter's cramp turned into a full-fledged charley horse.

"No?" Flemming pursed his lips to a pucker, then made a smacking sound. "I helped get Susan her role on 'Emergency Hospital.' And you know how that's done, don't you." He nodded at the infamous silver-brocaded couch. "She had marks on her back for a week."

Charley horse and all, Christopher leaped to his feet. The sales manager followed suit, keeping the slab of glass desk between them.

"And Lambert?" the reporter asked through teeth clenched against pain and frustration.

"Him, I never pimped for."

Christopher took hold of the transparent desktop and shoved it toward Flemming, pinning him against the wall.

"Hit me and you're fired," the salesman said, suddenly sounding unsure of himself. "You'll never be allowed back on this lot."

Now that was something Christopher couldn't afford. He let go of the glass and picked up the crystal pyramid. Hefting the knickknack, he decided it must weigh ten pounds at least. "Flemming, I hope you're a good catch."

But pinned as he was against the wall, the sales manager had little flexibility. The desktop shattered.

61

"Bad luck," Christopher said.

Only when he stepped outside the executive bungalow did the reporter allow himself the luxury of massaging his cramped leg. But any relief he felt faded beneath the onslaught of rain and doubt. What if Flemming had been speaking the truth?

Head bowed, he began hobbling toward the commissary, doing his best to concentrate on food. But for once, his stomach had met its match. Susan came before calories.

8

THE PINK GLOP quivered beneath Christopher's fork.

"Tasty looking, isn't it?" Brewster observed.

Not if you have to eat it, Christopher thought as he flashed his friend an inquiring glance.

In all apparent seriousness, Brewster added, "It's called 'Salad of the Stars.' The biggest damn thing to hit Hollywood in years. I had it added to the commissary menu especially for you."

Sure enough, the salad had been chalked on the executive menu board, which listed dishes available only to those sitting in the roped-off area of the dining room. Prices there were double the rest of the commissary, where everything was served cafeteria style. Waitresses, hoping to be discovered, worked the executive area.

"I'll have you know," Brewster said, his mouth full of mashed potatoes and gravy, "that dish of yours is copyrighted. I'll probably be sued."

As far as Christopher could see without actually tastetesting, the salad was nothing more than a rosy-colored blop of yogurt resting on a bed of curly lettuce, topped with alfalfa sprouts and peanuts. It was the dressing, however, that caught the attention of his nose. Pure vinegar by the smell of it and sour enough to curdle an anchorman's heart.

"I hear tell that Robert Redford lost forty pounds on Salad of the Stars," the station manager said.

"Redford's thin."

"That's what I mean. It must work. Besides, it will make a nice change of color for you, Bob."

Christopher stuck out his tongue.

"Still green," Brewster observed as he dug into a hot

63

beef sandwich covered in the commissary's all-purpose gravy, the smell of which brought back memories of Christopher's high school cafeteria. The reporter immediately began salivating.

"Eat up, Bob. All you want. I'm told no matter how much of that salad you eat, you can't possibly gain weight."

Christopher liberated a minuscule forkful, then chewed gingerly. The yogurt surprised him. He'd expected something sweet, a contrast to the vinegary dressing. What he got was a taste astringent enough to clot blood.

"I guess I'm not hungry," he announced, abandoning his fork to sink slowly into the pink blob.

"See what I mean? You stick with this diet and that waistline of yours will be back under control in no time." Brewster finished off his gravy-laden potatoes before adding what he must have thought was his ultimate enticement. "Just keep remembering how slim Susan is."

That did it. The reporter hated intimidation. He waved at a passing waitress, intending to overdose on chocolate. But she passed him by for Bill Bowzer's large, fan-packed table in the corner.

"Maybe a station manager can get service in here," Christopher grumbled.

A mere nod of Brewster's head brought another waitress.

"Mr. Christopher would like to order something else."

"Certainly." She smiled expectantly.

The bite of Christopher's belt buckle brought him to his senses. "Iced tea," he said meekly.

The waitress didn't leave until Brewster added, "Nothing for me, thank you."

Christopher sighed.

"Knock off twenty pounds, Bob, and I'll guarantee you an anchor slot. Maybe not a top position like Aarons, but something with enough exposure to make you a star. That's the way to get service around here. But this is nothing." He spread his hands to indicate the commissary, perhaps even the lot. "Imagine what it's like in New York."

"I don't want to be another Al Aarons."
"Hell, I don't blame you. I'm not crazy about the man either. But I'd make a deal with the devil to get to the Big Apple. And once I'm there, I won't forget my friends. That's a promise."
"What about here and now?"
The station manager compressed his lips into a tight line. "Here it comes. You want something, don't you?"
"I talked to Ed Flemming a few minutes ago."
"So I understand. Glass could be heard breaking all over the bungalow."
"I'll pay for it."
"For what? There were no witnesses."
"Wyn, I need you here. I won't last a day if you go to New York."
"Bite your tongue."
Christopher settled for a swallow of iced tea. "I'm still trying to find out what happened to Irma O'Donnell. That's why I went after Flemming. Something's not right there. Why the hell was he out in the rain at the time of the accident? Why wouldn't he do an interview during Sweeps?"
The reporter licked his lips and grimaced at the residue taste of yogurt. "I was only trying to get some answers."
"That's not what Flemming says."
"And what's that?"
"That Susan's made you crazy."
Christopher couldn't argue with that.
"That you're using the old woman's death to justify your own jealousy."
"So I'm gaga about her. But that won't stop me from doing my job."
"Just as long as you do your bit for 'The Six O'Clock News' during Sweeps I'll be happy. But you still haven't told me what it is you want from me right now."
Carte blanche will do, Christopher thought. But he couldn't ask for something like that without confessing that his "Six O'Clock" reports were canned, holdovers on tape that were not up to Sweeps standards. Before he

65

could open his mouth, however, Al Aarons made a grand entrance. Once inside the dining room, the anchorman stood poised, surveying the executive area and, if he ran true to form, assessing his chances of finding an important luncheon companion who might also pick up the tab. AA took a step toward Bowzer's corner, then apparently thought better of it and homed in on the station manager.

"Just remember," Brewster said under his breath, "New York depends on Aarons's ratings. So be nice."

Like an obedient soldier, Christopher bounced to his feet and clapped Aarons on the back. The maneuver brought a sigh from Brewster, while AA settled for an uneasy look of suspicion.

In answer to Brewster's pleading gesture, the reporter gave Aarons an opening. "How do you think Sweeps are going, Al?"

The anchorman didn't hesitate for a moment. Of course, Christopher had heard it all before. Aarons wanted less news and more time for himself.

To avoid further argument and the deadly glare coming from Brewster, Christopher kept a smile on his face, but he tuned out. As he did so, his gaze came to rest on Bingo Bradford, who had somehow managed to slip into the commissary unnoticed. The tape editor had joined the Bowzer table, where he was sitting right next to the master of ceremonies. With their heads together as they were, they looked like old friends. But what could two such men possibly have in common other than their initials?

"Excuse me," the reporter said.

Aarons, not missing a beat, kept right on talking.

Christopher pushed back his chair and got up. In answer to the stricken, trapped look on Brewster's face, the reporter mouthed, "Think of New York."

Then he hurried over to Bowzer's table. As host of ABN's most popular game show, Bill Bowzer was a force to be reckoned with. His "Bowzer Bags" had become part of the language, filled as they were with money.

Like so many other television MC's, Bowzer was slightly

past his prime, but still handsome enough to appeal to middle-aged females, which was the whole idea. He had always gone out of his way to be friendly to Christopher in the past, no doubt hoping for publicity, though never actually asking for it.

"Make room for Bobbo," Bowzer sang out to one of his production assistants, all of whom were female, all smitten, and all pretty enough to make a reporter regret his intemperate stomach.

With a glaring pout at Christopher, the woman on Bowzer's right vacated her chair and stalked from the commissary.

Once seated, the reporter was introduced to the other members of Bowzer's entourage: a network PR man, four fans who'd won the privilege of lunching with their hero, still another production assistant, and Bingo. The seating arrangement kept Bowzer between Christopher and the tape editor.

Leaning forward to peer around the show host, Christopher grinned evilly at Bingo, who immediately tucked himself closer to the table as if seeking shelter.

"Bingo's been explaining the intricacies of videotape to my guests," Bowzer explained with a wave toward his fans. "I thought they'd enjoy meeting one of television's real people, the ones who work behind the scenes."

The guilty look on Bingo's face didn't go with Bowzer's explanation.

"I'd like to hear that," the reporter said.

"That's the spirit, Bobbo." Bowzer nodded enthusiastically. "You know what I always say about this business. It pays to be humble, because you never know who might be the next head of the network."

At times like this, the game show host seemed too good to be true. His face shone with that candor you see radiating from TV evangelists, sincerity so intense you can't help wondering what's rotten underneath.

"In the end it all comes down to faith," Bowzer went on. "Take my friends here." He indicated the winners

67

from "Wheeler-Dealers." "They had faith. They selected one of my Bowzer Bags. That kind of trust won them twenty-five thousand dollars."

The faithful in question looked embarrassed. Perhaps they still couldn't believe their luck, that they had reached the grand prize plateau on "Wheeler-Dealers," a feat earning them a choice between a new car and a Bowzer Bag. The catch was that the bags contained anywhere from twenty-five cents to twenty-five thousand dollars.

"People like these are the reason I stay in this business," the show host declared. "Their good faith helps renew my own belief, my own—"

"What about Bingo?" Christopher interrupted.

At the question, the tape editor twitched violently. There was a clatter of falling objects beneath the table.

Christopher bent down in time to see the last of a pile of videotapes tumble from Bingo's lap. Instantly, the man was on hands and knees scooping up his treasures. But not before the reporter got a look at some of the labels, the same kind that were on the tape in Mark Lambert's dressing room.

Bingo banged his head getting out from under the table. But that didn't stop him from sprinting for the door, his cassettes clutched precariously against his chest.

Christopher was about to take off in hot pursuit when his beeper sounded. Suddenly all eyes in the commissary were on him as Gossett's sharp voice cut through the stillness. "Reisner's dreams have come true. Houses are sliding into the sea in Malibu."

Bingo would have to wait.

9

By the time Christopher returned to the lot, "The Eleven O'Clock News" was only a memory. And so was his last meal. Most restaurants in that area of East Hollywood had closed long ago, but tell that to his stomach.

The best he could do was ransom an icy hot dog from one of the vending machines. The microwave, usually out of order, worked well enough to turn his bun into the consistency of toothpaste. Even so, he managed to wash it down with a diet soda, followed immediately by indigestion. Loosening his belt failed to help, so he headed for the best couch in the building.

Once stretched out in the news director's office, Christopher sighed and tried to forget that heart attacks sometimes masquerade as indigestion. He forced himself to focus on the THINK MEAN plaque on the wall.

When Reisner had first nailed the slogan in place, Christopher had believed the man to be serious. But with the passage of time, the reporter had become convinced that the plaque was merely a prop, Reisner's way of reminding himself that only truly mean executives survived in television.

With that thought, Christopher closed his eyes and began to relax.

The next thing he knew Reisner was shaking him and shouting, "You're in my spot!"

"For God's sake, it's after midnight, Herb."

"Twenty-four hours a day this is mine. I don't rent it out." He grabbed hold of Christopher and began tugging.

"Why don't you go home?" the reporter said as he allowed himself to be pulled from the leather haven.

"Home. During Sweeps? Are you crazy? Do you know

how much pressure I've been getting?" Reisner was panting. "Wyn Brewster wants to be number one so badly he can taste it. But what he's tasting is my blood. So that's why I'm here, trying to come up with some new angle for tomorrow's news."

"It's still raining."

"People are getting tired of the same old disaster."

"I'll give you a piece on Irma O'Donnell."

Reisner screamed.

"I just want to help, Herb."

"If you mean that, give up the old lady and concentrate on something real, something I can use to get Brewster off my back."

"Think mean, Herb."

"Out!" Reisner bellowed.

With a weary grunt, Christopher left the office, consoled by the fact that at least his indigestion was gone. The newsroom was deserted, except for the overnight man, Hap Taylor, who looked busy for once. But then Reisner was still in the building.

Outside, rain ran down his neck and started him shivering. The quickest way to warmth was a high-calorie binge. Visions of fudge brownies blinded him as he ran full tilt into Father John, who himself was dashing across the lot with his head down against the elements.

"What brings you back among the dead?" greeted the priest as soon as they both recovered their balance. "Not the overnight again, I hope."

He referred to Christopher's temporary exile to the dark hours after a heated argument with Reisner. The banishment ended when the ratings began to slip.

"Mud slides and Irma O'Donnell," Christopher replied.

The priest sobered. "Yes, I heard about her. Such a lonely woman. I wish I could have helped."

"How did you know her?"

"Our paths crossed here in the dead hours."

Christopher felt gooseflesh creep along his spine.

Father John reached out. "Are you ill?"

The reporter shook his head. Then, almost as if he were confessing, he recounted his meeting with Irma O'Donnell.

In response the priest said, "I remember her so clearly. She was always clutching at that St. Christopher of hers. She wanted my help to get him reinstated." Father John spread his hands. "All I could do was try to redirect her zeal."

He sighed. "The church cannot afford to lose people of such faith. But I couldn't convince her to leave well enough alone. Stubborn, she was, but a good woman nevertheless."

The priest paused. His fingers intertwined. "Strange now that I think about it." He closed his eyes as if to focus on the memory. "She was grasping that medal of hers for all she was worth the last time we talked. And there were tears in her eyes."

Father John opened his eyes. He, too, had tears.

"She told me she had committed mortal sins," he said. "And because of them she was condemned to hell."

10

SINS OF THE night before had caught up with Christopher. Half a dozen fudge brownies had made it impossible to buckle his belt and drive at the same time. His stomach didn't have that much fold to it.

For comfort's sake he'd also kept his zipper at half staff while behind the wheel, despite the unnerving draft, which didn't let up even when he'd come to a complete stop on the ABN lot.

With a curse, he sucked in his stomach and attacked his belt. Yet struggle as he would, he couldn't fasten it while sitting down. He pounded the steering wheel in frustration and peered out at the rain, which was coming down beyond anything windshield wipers had ever been designed to handle.

Finally, taking a deep breath to steel himself, Christopher lurched out into the downpour. Since he couldn't handle an umbrella and his pants at the same time, water immediately soaked his head. He squirmed and fidgeted, while doing his best to keep his back to the rest of the parking lot. The last thing he needed was to be arrested as a flasher.

His hands, wet and cold enough to be partially numb, fumbled with the zipper. His shirttail snagged in the mechanism. When he yanked something ripped, but the embarrassing draft went away. However, the zipper was now stuck at the top. Eventually, he'd have to cut himself out of the trousers.

He had to expel every last bit of air from his lungs before he was able to secure the last notch of his belt, his danger notch. Just the hint of another calorie would put him over Reisner's limit. When that happened, there'd be fines and even the possibility of removal from the air. Of course, that was unlikely during Sweeps.

Vowing to avoid coffee or any other liquid that might force him to deal with his zipper prematurely, Christopher unfurled his umbrella and started across the lot toward the news building. When he was a hundred yards from his destination, a flock of "Wheeler-Dealers" descended upon him. They were being shepherded across the lot by half a dozen studio pages who had to constantly harangue their charges to keep them in order.

The sight turned Christopher giddy. Where was the yellow brick road? Where was reality?

Among the costumed hopefuls vying for spots on Bill Bowzer's game show, a giant chicken stretched and flapped its stubby wings.

Where did they find such people? The answer, of course, was to be found in Bowzer Bags. Why else would anyone stand around in the rain wetting their feathers?

Suddenly, Christopher had the feeling that he was the one in costume, the one out of step.

Like a traffic cop, one of the pages held up a hand signaling the reporter to stay where he was until the "Wheeler-Dealers" had passed. But the costumed crowd had other ideas. They surrounded Christopher and swept him along.

Nearby, the chicken cackled experimentally.

"You'll have to do better than that," Napoleon told him.

The chicken cackled again.

"No good."

Superman agreed.

The fowl fingered his papier mâché beak and crowed like a rooster.

"Wrong sex," Superman observed.

"Wait a minute," Napoleon said. "Maybe he's got something there. They just might go for a queer bird."

Superman started to laugh, then appeared to think better of it. He moved away. When time came for the show's producers to pick final contestants, they seldom selected two from the same location in the crowd. So suddenly no one wanted to stand next to the chicken. It tried to reassure them with a phony sounding cackle. When that didn't work, the bird shrugged its sodden feathers at Christopher, who was doing his best to fend off a vampire with snapping plastic teeth.

Overhead, the midday sky suddenly let go with a vengeance. The rain was gone, replaced by something Noah would have been proud of. A couple of minutes in such weather and not even the heartiest costume would be fit for air.

Realizing that, the pages began running their charges toward the nearest shelter, the news building. Once inside, the contestants were lined up against a corridor wall to keep them out of the way. It also gave the pages the opportunity to sort their charges by category—historical figures in one group, movie tie-ins in another. The chicken, Christopher noticed, was herded in with a barnyard bunch, including Mother Goose, a cow, and two ends of a horse.

Dazed, Christopher fell into line next to the chicken, who immediately shrank away as if the reporter's civilian clothes might jeopardize all game-show chances. Poor bastard, Christopher thought. "Wheeler-Dealers" had had its fill of chickens in recent weeks.

Of course, no one but Bowzer knew exactly how contestants were picked. Sometimes innovation alone did the trick. At others, only those making complete fools of themselves would be chosen. Which meant Christopher was a certainty if he stayed where he was.

As the reporter was about to take flight, producers arrived. But they passed him by. Even the chicken clucked its condolences.

And then suddenly came shouts as one finalist after another was selected.

The reporter saw Napoleon being led from the building sheltered under a massive umbrella. Next came Julius Caesar. Perhaps this particular segment of "Wheeler-

Dealers" was to be an all-military show. But selection of Superman put an end to such speculation. Besides, ABN had a Superman movie coming up, which Bill Bowzer could now promote on his show with apparent legitimacy.

Once the last of the finalists had been taken away, the pages went back to work, driving everyone else back outside. The chicken, however, managed to dodge out of line unnoticed. It immediately fled up a stairway leading to the newsroom and executive offices. The chicken's manner was not that of someone merely fleeing the rain. Rather, its skulking movements reminded Christopher of someone trying to sneak in somewhere without paying.

A triumphant cackle echoed down the stairway.

Intrigued, Christopher was about to give chase when Robin Flick latched onto his arm.

"Take pity," "Vision" 's producer said. "I need help getting upstairs."

Never before had she so much as smiled at him. But then she had her sights set higher than a lowly reporter.

"Bad grass," she explained, her eyes closing down to the merest slits. "Probably sprayed with paraquat, or whatever it is the narcs use these days. No doubt I'll go blind."

She licked her bright red lips. Despite her pitiful pleas, she didn't look any the worse for wear. Her makeup was immaculate, her clothes, though dry, clung wetly in just the right places.

Christopher closed his eyes for a moment. Then he blinked and started briskly up the stairs. But she anchored him like a dead weight.

"It seems awfully bright in here," she said.

He glanced back at the doorway through which the last of the "Wheeler-Dealers" had disappeared. At best, the light filtering in from outside was a dull gray.

"It's that show of mine," Robin went on. "It's turning me into a creature of the night. I've got to get off that shift."

She took a couple of experimental steps toward the

second floor. After two more strides she was breathing heavily. By the time they reached the first landing, she was moaning. "My God, I'll never make it."

Though he tried to keep her moving, she refused to budge. "Let me catch my breath at least."

"It's a chicken I want to catch," Christopher said.

On the next step lay a huge yellow feather.

Robin blinked several times. "That does it. No more pills. I don't care what they are." With a soft groan she stooped to pick up the plume. In her grasp, the paper feather collapsed into a sodden mess. For some reason, she looked terribly cheated, as if it had been a prize suddenly denied her. She squeezed the debris into a ball and hurled it against the wall, where is stuck like a lump of modern sculpture. Then, producing still another groan, she tackled the second flight of stairs.

Outside Aarons's door they paused, Robin sucking air and psyching herself like an athlete getting ready to do battle. Within seconds her bearing changed. Her face took on new life. She was bright-eyed and wide awake, though trembling, the price she paid for mixing adrenaline and pills.

"Is Aarons worth it?" Christopher asked.

"I don't believe people like you. He's the main anchor on both the 'Six' and 'Eleven O'Clock,' for God's sake. A man like that can make my career."

"In case you hadn't noticed, you're still living in 'Vision's Sunday morning ghetto."

"Not for long," she said. "Watch me." With that she took a deep breath and sounded, "Charge!"

She flung open the door without knocking.

Aarons took one look at her and uttered an obscene proposition. Then he saw the reporter and winked broadly to cover his discomfort.

"Alfie," Robin cooed, "I want to talk to you."

"Alfie?" Christopher asked, unable to suppress a grin.

"We'd like to be alone," the anchorman declared.

"Let him stay," Robin said. "I may need a witness."

Aarons's eyes flared to klieg-light intensity, but he said nothing.

Robin stroked his cheek. "It's 'Vision,' Alfie. The hours are killing me."

Aarons looked stubborn.

"Of course," Robin added, "I could always sleep afternoons. But then we wouldn't see much of each other, would we?"

The anchorman obviously didn't like that idea. As Christopher well knew, afternoons were his only free time.

"And no matter how hard I work," Robin went on, "it doesn't seem to make any difference. Nobody watches Sunday morning TV. I'm not getting anywhere."

"You've made it as far as my couch," Aarons said sarcastically.

Christopher wanted to leave, but the producer held him fast. Aarons's remark had brought a flush to Robin's face, but she didn't back down.

"If afternoons are out, maybe we could meet after the late news," she suggested coyly.

Aarons's wife expected him home promptly after the eleven o'clock news broadcast.

"There must be some alternative," he said, sending a sickly smile in Christopher's direction. "Come here and we'll talk about it." He dropped onto the couch and patted the cushion next to him, but his voice lacked enthusiasm. "Exactly what do you want from me?"

"I've been thinking about moving to the news department. That's where the action is." She turned to Christopher. "Don't you think so, Bobby?"

"Of course."

"As what?" Aarons said warily.

"I could start out as a writer. That seems simple enough."

"*My* writers have years of experience. Most of them have degrees in journalism."

"How about producer then? I wouldn't have to write." With a nod she appealed to Christopher.

The reporter held up a hand. "I don't do the hiring around here."

Robin leaned toward Aarons and licked her lips, a deliberate, sensual ploy. "I'm sure if you asked Reisner as a personal favor, he'd put me on staff."

AA ran his fingers around the rims of his ears, a gesture that revealed his expensive toupee. "If I do that, I'll owe him one."

"Think of what you owe me."

There was a pounding on the door.

"Who is it?" Aarons called out.

The pounding intensified.

"Go away," the anchorman shouted.

The only response was more pounding.

Muttering obscenities, Aarons lunged for the door. The instant he opened it, the chicken thrust itself over the threshold. Surprised, the anchorman backed away until he bumped into Christopher.

The bird, soaking wet, cocked its dripping head to one side and studied the anchorman with a single eye. Then it let out a clucking sound, something akin to a *tut-tut* of disapproval.

"If this is some kind of publicity stunt," Aarons said, "you can forget Channel 3."

The chicken cackled and waved a wing toward the couch. "I see you're up to your old pornographic tricks." The male voice sounded familiar.

"What's going on?" Christopher demanded.

The bird jumped as if seeing the reporter for the first time, pulled a metal chair over to the door, then ducked back beyond the threshold and slammed the door behind it.

"What have you been telling people?" Aarons screamed at Robin.

Before she had time to answer, the anchorman surged forward, flung open the door, and banged his shins on the metal chair. With a curse, Aarons tossed aside the flimsy barricade and ran after the fleeing bird, Christopher right behind him.

"Maybe a career switch to the news department isn't such a good idea," Robin called after them.

Christopher's pounding heart reminded him that he wasn't getting any younger. But he'd be damned if he'd give up the chase. That chicken had some explaining to do before it got its neck wrung.

Ahead of him, Aarons panted to a stop. He'd come to a crossroads. Directly in front of him was the entrance to the newsroom. Off to the left ran a long hall that ended at Reisner's office. The other way led out of the building.

The anchorman leaned against the wall to catch his breath. "That chicken's given us the slip," he gasped. In frustration he kicked the plaster. That was when he noticed a feather on the tiled floor. The plume pointed straight toward the news director's office.

As quietly as possible, he tiptoed toward Reisner's closed door. There, he paused, panting raggedly.

He swallowed once, twice, then managed to speak in a sort of quiet croak. "That bird's in there spilling its gizzard right now."

"About what?" Christopher asked.

Unsteadily, the anchorman reached out and took hold of the knob again. He was about to open the door when a sound of crowing came from the other end of the hall.

Both men turned in time to see the chicken emerging from the newsroom. It flapped its wing at them, a wing carrying a package, then took off around a corner, back toward Aarons's office once again.

With an exhausted gesture, the anchorman waved Christopher after the fleeing figure.

What the hell, the reporter decided, and gave chase. As he turned the corner, he saw that he was gaining on the bird, who was now having trouble with its footing on the asphalt tile.

79

Thank God for crepe soles, the reporter thought, and speeded up.

At the head of the stairs, Christopher made a grab for tail feathers, but the chicken vaulted out of reach. By the time the reporter reached the outside door, the bird had exited into a driving rain heavy enough to destroy even the best of intentions.

Clenching his teeth in frustration, Christopher banged his head softly against the glass door as he watched the chicken disappear down an alley that led in the direction of the props department.

Then, feeling exhausted, the reporter retraced his steps toward Aarons's office. Perhaps someone had been playing a practical joke. If so, that bird should have laid an egg instead of the bombshell about pornography.

What it had done was leave a package outside the anchorman's door, a package that Aarons was now nudging gingerly with the toe of his shoe. As soon as he saw Christopher, AA scooped up the parcel and disappeared into his office.

11

PACING BENEATH HIS "Think Mean" plaque, Herb Reisner pleaded with Christopher. "The overnights came in. We dropped a rating point. If we lose another, I'll be working in Pocatello."

The reporter moved his chair back out of the way so the news director had plenty of room to work off his aggression. "I take it," Christopher said, "you've been getting pressure from the brass."

"Ed Flemming paid me a personal visit. You should consider his interest flattering. He thinks we need more of you on the air to boost our ratings. He wants you live every half hour during the news. What do you think about that?"

"What do you, Herb?"

"That Flemming is meeting with the station manager right now. If he gets his way, my friend, you'll have no time for Irma O'Donnell or anything else for that matter. She will be one of your crusades that didn't work out."

"Brewster will back me."

"But for how long? Until tomorrow's overnight comes in? Besides, you—we—can't afford to have Flemming as an enemy. He's sure to step up to station manager when Brewster leaves."

"Have you heard something I haven't?"

"It's no secret that Brewster wants a network slot. Sooner or later we're going to have to deal with Ed Flemming. In the end, the sales department always wins."

"What's the climate like in Pocatello?"

"Too cold for our thin California blood."

The reporter shivered theatrically.

"With each rating point worth more than a million bucks, Flemming isn't going to let you stand in the way."

"The fabled million-dollar point," Christopher murmured with mock awe. "There's never been a TV station yet that lost money. When the FCC grants a license, it's a license to steal."

"I haven't got the time to discuss morality with you. I just wanted to warn you that you'll be going back to work shortly." The news director pursed his lips. "And what about that diet of yours? You look over the limit to me."

"Don't try changing the subject, Herb, not until I've found out why Irma was killed. After that, you can weigh me."

"Total starvation might be the best solution." Reisner rubbed his eyes, which were beginning to water. "Have you ever thought about going to a fat farm?"

Christopher studied the news director, whose left eye lost all sense of coordination when the pressure got too great. At the moment, the orb was rolling viciously, threatening to run amok.

"Christopher, you're a—"

A shriek put an end to further discussion.

"That sounds like Aarons," Reisner snapped and charged from the office with Christopher in pursuit.

A second shriek, more pitiful than the first, confirmed the news director's appraisal. AA was in trouble.

The artificial hairs on the anchorman's head were standing straight out, the result of his tugging at them frantically. It was a miracle the adhesive hadn't let go already.

Reisner grabbed hold of Aarons. But AA, in his present state, was too much for him.

"Dammit, Christopher," Reisner grunted, "give me a hand."

Together, they managed to pin the flailing anchorman to the floor. Face down on the carpet, he stopped struggling and went limp. Nap-deadened sobs wracked his body.

The news director made soothing noises, like a parent reassuring a small child.

Christopher was used to the anchorman's tantrums, but this kind of breakdown made the reporter wonder if he hadn't misjudged the man. Perhaps he wasn't what he had seemed. Perhaps he didn't mean the things he said, that reporters were a lower form of life, one from which he'd had the good sense to evolve. Or that writers and producers were Martians. Among news personnel, Aarons treated only Reisner as an equal. But Christopher knew that would stop once the ratings improved, once the anchorman had enough million-dollar points stacked up to make himself invulnerable.

But for the moment, the reporter felt sorry for AA, who turned over to reveal red eyes and a lint-covered nose.

Finally, the news director's murmurings began to take effect. The sobs subsided, though the tears continued. Christopher offered a handkerchief, which Aarons could only accept after Reisner unpinned his arms.

AA honked several times before getting himself under control enough to gasp, "The chicken."

"The chicken?" Reisner repeated dumbly, like a straight man in a comedy routine.

"Not a real chicken," the anchorman clarified.

"I saw it too," Christopher said.

"You see," Aarons bleated. "I'm not imagining things."

"A 'Wheeler-Dealer,' " Christopher added. "Maybe."

"Tell us about the chicken," the news director suggested, his tone placating.

The anchorman's hands fluttered to his head, where they discovered the toupee's disarray. Adeptly, fingers began smoothing the synthetics back into place.

"We want to help," Reisner said.

Aarons's eyes blazed suddenly, as if key lights had just been switched on. But after a moment, the sparkle diminished and he began explaining his encounter with the chicken.

"So we've got a nut wearing a bird suit," Reisner summed up. "Well, don't worry about it. I'll notify security. If you like, we'll post a man on your door."

83

Aarons shook his head. "You don't understand." With obvious effort he got unsteadily to his feet and moved to the video tape machine that was shelved beneath his twenty-five-inch TV set. Carefully, he extracted a cassette. "The chicken left this."

Torn wrapping paper from the chicken's gift lay on the floor nearby.

Aarons handled the cassette as if it were an egg.

Christopher already had a good idea what was on the tape.

"It's enough to ruin me," Aarons said, confirming the reporter's deduction. "And Channel 3 will go down the drain right along with me."

Reisner, whose face had taken on a Pocatello-bound look, snatched the tape and quickly reloaded it for playback. But as soon as that was done, he hesitated, his finger hovering over the start button. Only after an audible sigh did he manage to stab the machine to life.

By the looks of the pornography, it was ancient. Certainly AA had been a much younger man, young enough to have had real hair on his head.

"An impressive performance," was all Christopher could think to say after viewing the montage of sexual feats.

"I was just a kid," the anchorman responded.

"Some childhood."

"All right, Christopher," Reisner snapped. "That isn't helping any." The news director turned back to his anchorman. "Where is it, Al?"

"Where's what?"

"You like watching yourself too much to have screamed at the sight of your misspent youth."

Christopher looked at his boss with new respect. The man was more than a mere executive; he had the instincts of a reporter.

Aarons was blubbering again, an obvious attempt to duck answering the news director's question.

"The blackmail note," Christopher guessed, wondering if it was really as simple as that.

"Twenty-five thousand dollars," AA blurted. "Otherwise copies of that tape go to every tabloid in the country."

"They'll never get printed," Reisner declared, though he didn't sound all that certain. "The ABN lawyers will see to that."

"They won't have to print them. Once those rags start calling me an ex-porno star, it's all over. Viewers want their newsmen lily-white."

Aarons blew his nose, then held the handkerchief out to Christopher.

The reporter didn't really want it back. "Fans have a forgiving nature," he said, ignoring the offering. "They like to think their idols have a human side."

The anchorman sniffled. "It will never be the same. Nobody will take me seriously. My credibility will be gone."

Reisner looked as if he could use a handkerchief too. "I won't even be able to find work in Pocatello." He reached for the phone like a man in pain. "I'd better let Wyn Brewster know that we're on our way to Idaho."

When the station manager joined them, he listened attentively, the expression on his face reminding Christopher that to Brewster, Los Angeles was Pocatello. Finally he said, "Twenty-five thousand is little enough to pay if it stops there. I just hope I can get the network to see things the same way."

"I don't see why not," Christopher blurted. "It's no more than a full Bowzer bag."

Brewster answered with a glare, then stepped close to Aarons, who was again playing finger games with his toupee. "Frankly, Al, I don't have any choice in this matter. If I don't back you, all our work, our Sweeps promotion, will go down the toilet. Hell, an anchor change now would set us back months and who knows how many rating points."

AA's watery eyes narrowed. "Does that mean I won't have to pay out of my own pocket?"

"What are the exact instructions for delivering the money?" Brewster asked.

Aarons handed over the blackmail note, which the station manager then read out loud, his voice betraying no emotion. According to the chicken's demands, the money was to be placed in a brown paper bag and given to one of the studio pages assigned to "Wheeler-Dealers." Sometime during the coming week the page would be approached and asked, "Is that my lunch you're holding?" The twenty-five thousand was then to be handed over.

"What about the police?" Christopher asked.

Brewster shook his head. "If we let them in on this, the competition will get wind of it sure as hell. We can't afford that in the middle of Sweeps."

"I don't agree. This has to be connected with Irma O'Donnell. Otherwise . . ."

The station manager held up a hand for silence. "I'm not saying we keep this from the police permanently, but just until after the ratings are in. Hell, Bob, if I thought telling them Al's face was on that tape would solve anything, I'd show it to them right now."

"You're forgetting one thing," Christopher added. "There's no reason that chicken couldn't have masqueraded as a surgeon. And that makes him a murderer."

Aarons went so pale his lips looked purple. "Are you saying I could have been killed by that bird?"

"Christopher is only guessing," Brewster said. "Besides, you're the goose. Nobody is going to kill you before you lay the golden egg."

12

BILL BOWZER RATED a suite in the executive bungalow. To get to his inner sanctum, you had to cross his secretary's vast office, itself luxurious enough to make an anchorman weep, and proceed down a hallway hung with costumes from past "Wheeler-Dealer" shows.

Ignoring Donald Duck, Attila the Hun, and a large golden angel, Christopher burst in upon Bowzer unannounced. At first the reporter could see nothing in the darkened office but naked bodies blazing from a giant TV screen that took up an entire wall. But almost immediately, Christopher's eyes adjusted to take in the illuminated faces of Bowzer and Bingo Bradford, their mouths slack as they leered up at the writhing flesh.

The reporter's arrival filled the office with light from the hallway.

"Dammit, Janice," Bowzer blurted, "I told you I didn't want to be disturbed."

"Your secretary is out to lunch," Christopher said, switching on the lights.

Both men squinted blindly for a moment, then Bingo leaped to kill the video tape. The sixty-inch screen, a prize eventually destined for "Wheeler-Dealers," faded to a glow. There'd been no sign of Al Aarons in the orgy.

"How's business?" the reporter asked Bingo.

In answer, the tape editor swiveled his head toward Bowzer, who quickly said, "This is a private meeting."

Christopher ignored the MC. "The last time I saw you, Bingo, you were dressed as a chicken." It was a guess, but worth a try.

Instead of replying, the tape editor concentrated on

removing the video cassette from the playback mechanism.

The reporter turned to Bowzer. "Pornography is being used to blackmail someone on this lot."

"I . . ." He took a deep breath and rubbed his reddening face. Then he said to Bingo, "I think you'd better explain what's going on."

The tape editor pulled down his Dodgers' cap. Then, without warning, he charged into Bowzer, sending the man crashing into Christopher. Both of them went down in a heap while the tape editor made good his escape, careening down the hall so recklessly that he swept the golden angel from the wall.

Impact with the sharp edge of Bowzer's desk cracked Christopher's knee. Pain blinded him momentarily; there was no question of immediate pursuit. All he could do was roll on the floor and curse. After a long while, he allowed Bowzer to give him a hand up.

Once on his feet, Christopher clenched his teeth to ask, "How long have you been doing business with Bingo?"

"I don't do business with *him*. The fact is, this was the first time the man was ever in my office." He tugged at the sleeve of his immaculate blue blazer, then smoothed his white ducks.

"Were you buying or renting?" Christopher asked, studying the wall behind Bowzer's desk, where a floor-to-ceiling bookcase contained leatherbound classics.

When no answer was forthcoming, the reporter said, "People have died on this lot, deliberately murdered as far as I'm concerned. And now there's blackmail, with Bingo Bradford and his pornography popping up everywhere I turn. And you seem to be right in the middle."

"The man tried to sell me something. I gave him the courtesy of looking."

"And what did you see?"

"Nothing I haven't seen before." Bowzer looked away for a moment, unable to meet the reporter's steady gaze. Then, with a sigh, the MC went eye-to-eye. "I'm telling the truth. The only other contact I've ever had with Bradford was once at that bingo game of his. And I only played then to show my crew that I was a regular guy. In this business, a man can't afford to make enemies of technicians. You know how easy it is to sabotage a career. An open mike, maybe. Technical error, they call it, but you and I know better."

The next thing Christopher knew, Bowzer would be crying like a baby. Yet the reporter saw no reason why he shouldn't believe the man. After all, he had an annual salary rumored to be in excess of a million dollars. So what possible reason could he have for risking his career for cheap blackmail?

"God is my witness," Bowzer continued. "I know it's unfashionable these days, but I believe in God. It's the one reason I keep doing my show year after year. Certainly I don't need the money. The fact is I could retire right now and never have to worry about another thing the rest of my life." He paused for a dramatic shake of his head. "No, that's a lie. I would worry. I'd worry about the people who need me, who without me would have no joy in their lives."

He hesitated, his face glistening with sweat. "You see, Christopher, it's God's work I do."

With a flourish, he hefted a bulging Bowzer Bag from a desk drawer. "I know everybody on the lot makes jokes about these. Bowzer's Doggie bags, they call them. But I don't care. I feed souls with these."

Bowzer held out the bag. "For your soul."

The reporter backed away.

"Go ahead," Bowzer urged. "Take it."

Christopher made no move to accept the offering.

"I insist," the man said, stepping forward to thrust the bag against Christopher's stomach.

The contents had sharp edges.

"You thought it was money, didn't you? Well, I can't blame you. Go ahead, open it up and take a look for yourself."

89

The bag contained religious tracts. When Christopher tried to give it back, Bowzer clasped his hands behind his back. The man looked smug as hell.

"Exactly what was Bingo trying to sell you?" Christopher asked.

"He claimed to have come up with a tape featuring someone famous. Of course, it was going to be expensive, or so he said."

"How much?"

"We never got around to that."

With a sigh, Christopher returned the tracts to the open desk drawer. "I need a favor."

Bowzer, his hands rubbing together eagerly like Pilate out for a good scrub, smiled broadly and said, "For you, Bob, anything."

"I want to borrow a costume."

"Fans have sent me hundreds of them. The props department has closets full."

"I'd rather not deal with props."

"Okay. We've got plenty around here. I'll have my secretary find you something."

Christopher settled for the fallen angel.

13

FEELING ANYTHING BUT angelic, Christopher lay on his bed listening to his stomach rumble from too much acid and Irma O'Donnell. At times like this, he felt as if television were eating him alive.

Overhead, in the attic, the raccoons were munching on God knows what. Their loud crunching made him sit up and cock his head nervously. Perhaps they were feasting on electrical wiring. If so, he ought to do something. But what? All previous strategies had failed.

"Knock it off!" he shouted at the ceiling. Lame but better than nothing.

The crunching stopped, but only momentarily.

Christopher sighed. It was his own fault. When the pair of raccoons had first moved in by ripping a hole in the wood shingled roof, he had thought them charming. Of course, that was before the kits came, three of them, full-grown now and raising hell.

Twice in recent weeks he had tried to evict the family, a procedure requiring a nocturnal vigil to make certain they'd all left the attic in search of food. After that he'd nailed up their hole. And each time they'd ripped open a new patch of shingles, the last such excavation directly over his bedroom.

At the moment, he was staring up at the plaster, where an ugly yellow stain was growing by leaps and bounds.

"That had better be rain!" he yelled.

They answered with what sounded suspiciously like snorts of glee.

On the premise that what he couldn't see was a lot less worry, he closed his eyes and tried to relax. But Irma wouldn't permit it.

With a groan he blinked and sat up. If she wasn't going to let him sleep, he'd comfort himself with food, although he'd already had to buy a new belt.

The phone, like a sharp twinge from his conscience, startled him.

"Yes," he said tentatively, expecting Gossett or worse.

"I make house calls," Susan said in her doctor's voice.

Stunned, Christopher could only say, "Huh?"

"Don't take two aspirin. Don't take anything. I'm bringing dinner."

"Now?"

"You did ask me for a date, didn't you?"

Christopher nodded before managing to get out a throaty, "Yes."

"What's the address?"

He gave her the number in Pasadena. "I'm on the lip of arroyo not far from the Rose Bowl." And close enough, he thought, to occupy the burglars who sold their wares at the stadium's monthly flea market.

"No one lives on that side of Los Angeles."

"There's nothing like old money," he said.

"Well, I've used new money to buy this pizza."

"I'm on a diet."

"It's diet pizza. All you have to do is supply the wine. You do have wine, don't you?"

"We manage that even in Pasadena."

"I'll be there as soon as I can."

Susan lived in Beverly Hills. That gave him about forty-five minutes to get the place cleaned up.

He went crazy for half an hour, vacuuming the floor and washing dishes. Finally he was down to the big decision, whether or not to strip and change the bed. He told himself he was being foolish, that a woman as beautiful as Susan Arthur wanted an eating companion, nothing more. But the sound of her voice had turned him into an optimist. He rummaged around until he found his one spare set of sheets. While he struggled with hospital corners, the raccoons ran amok overhead.

"I hope Susan likes animals," he shouted at them. "Otherwise, out you go."

By the time the bed looked inviting, Christopher was sweating so badly that he had to shower. The doorbell rang while he was still toweling dry.

"I'll be right there," he called, pulling on a battered terry-cloth robe. At least, the fuzzy garment didn't look as if it were part of some suave seduction plan. Even so, he felt embarrassed answering the door like that. But all thought of apology left his head when Susan kissed him, her free hand pulling gently at the terry cloth nap. He didn't know which made him more giddy, the smell of her perfume or the aroma of pizza.

Breaking contact, she brandished the cardboard container and said, "Let's eat this before it gets any colder."

"As soon as I get dressed."

"Don't bother. You've got on as much as I do." She pulled at her "Emergency Hospital" T-shirt, which was stretched tight enough to make Christopher catch his breath. Her designer jeans didn't hide anything either. She wiggled out of her running shoes and headed for the kitchen, where she deposited the pizza on a countertop. More than ever, he was conscious of being ten years older than she was.

"Now where's the wine?" Susan asked.

As he was reaching up into a cupboard for it, she patted him playfully on the rump, causing him to juggle the bottle momentarily.

"Are you ticklish?" she said, unrolling several yards of paper towel to use as napkins.

Christopher's face flushed. "That wasn't exactly a tickle."

"Men pat women on the fanny all the time and think nothing of it. Why shouldn't I?" She smiled knowingly. "Didn't you like it?"

Instead of answering, he fished a slice of pizza from the box and bit off a mouthful.

"I got half with anchovies," she said, "half without."

It had been so long since Christopher had indulged in pizza that not even little dead fish could put him off.

"I just can't believe what's happening," Susan said between bites. "You know, at the studio. People dying and all that." She shivered, making her breasts jiggle provocatively.

Christopher had trouble swallowing.

She nibbled off an anchovy and chewed thoughtfully for a moment. "Somebody said you believe that Mark Lambert was murdered. That he didn't commit suicide."

Averting his eyes, he told her some of his reasons, among them pornographic video tape.

"Who'll be next?" Susan asked as if accepting his theory as gospel.

While speaking so earnestly, she looked very young and vulnerable. Yet she had been fighting for her professional life on the soaps for more than three years. No one vulnerable could have survived that kind of combat.

"There's no reason to think someone else will be killed," he said.

"Someone looking for a killer, someone like you, could be in danger." She stared down at an anchovy, made a face as if the sight of anything dead suddenly depressed her, then tossed the pizza slice back into the box. "I shouldn't eat this stuff anyway. A few more ounces on my hips and they'll write me out of the script."

Christopher eyed the hips in question. She looked perfect to him, but he knew that TV cameras added pounds.

He took another bite, wondering if he was unconsciously eating himself into another career. Maybe an out-of-control horizontal hold would put an end to his crusading once and for all.

"I'm getting morbid," Susan said suddenly, shaking herself. "But I know how to fix that."

From the back pocket of her jeans, she produced a small plastic bag filled with white powder. She winked and said, "Things go better with coke."

"I don't know how to tell you this, Susan, but I've never

tried it. And I don't think . . ." At the moment being straight embarrassed him.

"We use it all the time on the set. It keeps everybody relaxed. One snort of this and you'll see what I mean."

"You go ahead."

"Come on. What's life without a little sin?"

There'd been a time in Christopher's life when coffee was a sin. But that was what being brought up in Salt Lake City did to a person, even one who wasn't a Mormon. Coffee, tea, Coca-Cola, cigarettes, all were the sins of his youth. But when it came to hard drugs, he might as well have been one of Brigham Young's Latter-day Saints.

"I'll pass," he said.

"Try just a little, for me." Her tone was that of a mother wheedling a reluctant child. "I'll show you how to do it."

The skin-tight jeans gave up a small pocket mirror, on which she prepared the dosage. After snorting through a gold straw, she fixed another portion, smaller than her own. Then she beckoned him with a smile.

When he held back, she said, "This stuff makes sex fantastic."

Had such an offer come from anyone else, Christopher would have refused. But coming from Susan . . .

At first, he thought the drug wasn't working, that perhaps he was immune. But then euphoria set in and suddenly, as if there had been no time transition at all, he found himself in bed with the woman he'd been fantasizing about for months.

The outside world ceased to exist. His planet was Susan. He revolved around her like a worshiping moon. In heavenly cataclysm, he touched her.

There was an explosion, then a scream as the bedroom ceiling directly above them gave way. A terrified, snarling raccoon came crashing through the wet plaster.

Because of the cocaine, it all seemed to happen in slow motion. Time was so strung out there was no possibility of panic. Easily, as if he'd confronted frenzied raccoons every day of his life, Christopher herded the beast into the garage, which opened directly off the kitchen, and locked it inside.

Returning to bed, he saw Susan examining her thigh where the raccoon had bitten her.

"I'm going to have a scar," she said, emotion beginning to override the drug.

"You can always have a depraved patient written into the script," he said. His remark cheered her.

But by the time they arrived at the hospital, pain had sobered her to the point where she was glaring at Christopher as if he had personally planned the attack.

"And you a doctor," he said, trying to reestablish rapport.

But what the real doctor had to say ended all possibility of that. The raccoon had to be quarantined, otherwise Susan would have to undergo a series of painful rabies shots. After such a revelation, she had words for Christopher that he'd never heard from the lips of a lady before.

14

HALO WIRED SECURELY in place, Christopher felt like a guardian angel as he joined the ranks of the Wheeler-Dealers. Now all he had to do was keep one brown paper bag and one studio page in sight.

At first it was easy. But as more and more contestants swelled the crowd it became a constant battle for him to hold his position. The continuing rain didn't help any. Because of it, the Wheeler-Dealers were forced to huddle beneath a corrugated metal roof in one of the open-sided audience holding areas.

Several times the reporter had to jump up and down to see over the heads of the crush around him. Once he tried to shake free of the crowd entirely, but everyone seemed to think it good luck to stay close to an angel.

When a surgeon joined the throng, Christopher blinked as if seeing things. But the man's green operating garb, freshly laundered and starched, drew hoots of derision from those nearby.

"No imagination," said the front end of a cow.

The other end added a muffled, "A little fake blood might help."

Christopher ground his teeth. There'd been too much blood spilled already. But he said nothing, remaining quietly angelic behind his golden mask.

The surgeon, who wore dark glasses in addition to his operating mask, ignored the comments. In fact, as far as Christopher could see the man had eyes only for the brown paper bag, toward which the surgeon edged ever nearer.

For a moment the reporter lost sight of him. In that instant, all sorts of unlikely thoughts ran through Christopher's mind. But he comforted himself by thinking that a murderer wouldn't use the same disguise twice. Unless, of course, he was a genius, in which case he'd know that the last thing anyone would look for again would be a surgeon.

Christopher practically trampled a Viking god to get the surgeon in sight again. And that was the moment a masked nun emerged from behind an overblown Cleopatra to accost the page carrying the ransom.

The paper bag changed hands.

Instantly, the nun stepped out from under the corrugated roof. But the deluge didn't faze her as she dashed across a narrow studio street and into the ladies' room.

Removing his mask, Christopher charged after her.

The reporter's entrance to a packed house brought feminine screams of protest. He wagged his halo apologetically but knew his was a lost cause. The ladies loo was one place angels feared to tread. Besides, where could the nun go but out the door she'd gone into?

Back outside, Christopher waved frantically to attract the attention of studio security, which had been put on alert. But all the reporter succeeded in luring to his side was a bedraggled page, whose umbrella couldn't cope with the downpour.

"Mr. Christopher," the young man said. "Employees aren't eligible to become contestants on 'Wheeler-Dealers.' "

"Were you briefed on the brown paper bag?"

A look of pity was the only answer.

Exasperated, Christopher said, "Go to the executive bungalow, find Wyn Brewster, and tell him the man we want is hiding in the ladies' room." He pointed at the door through which a knot of women were now exiting. Since they wore no costumes, they must have been scheduled as members of the audience.

"Pervert!" one said.

Another smiled as if to say an angel in the Ladies was a refreshing experience. Could she be a nun in mufti? He hoped not.

"Is anything wrong?" the page asked the first woman.

"That man came inside. He's a Peeping Tom. He ought to be arrested."

The page eyed Christopher in a new light.

"The executive bungalow," the reporter reiterated. "And that's an order."

Even then, the young man hesitated.

"Please," Christopher said. "It's important."

Before leaving, the page called over one of his peers to keep an eye on the reporter.

"And if you can't find Brewster," Christopher added, "get the chief of security."

No sooner had the page disappeared in the direction of the bungalow than two elderly guards arrived. They looked much alike, old enough to be supplementing pensions, and both sporting bushy mustaches that drooped over their upper lips. One bushy growth was gray, the other a dark, gleaming black. "They call us Salt and Pepper," said the one with the gray bristles. "I'm Salt."

As soon as Christopher explained the situation, Pepper was quick to say, "We were told to keep an eye on that kid with the bag."

"But in all this rain," Salt went on, "we lost track of him."

"Our orders were to remain unobtrusive." Pepper pronounced this last word as if he'd memorized it especially for the occasion.

"Oh, hell," Christopher said. "One of you stay here and grab the nun if she gets by us. The other come inside with me."

The reporter cracked open the door and called, "Anybody inside?"

"Yes," came a female reply.

"Men coming in," Christopher declared and did just that.

A wide-eyed woman scuttled past him and out the door, which Salt held for her.

That left the two men alone. Christopher checked the

99

stalls, found them empty, and was baffled until he saw the loose grating over an air duct. Angrily, he jerked off the covering and peered into a dark tunnel big enough to hold nun or angel.

"I'm too old for climbing around in there," Salt said. "And don't let that mustache of Pepper's fool you. He's no spring chicken either."

Taking a deep breath, Christopher stepped into the duct. Metal groaned under foot. At the first junction, there was no choice but to turn right. Once done, darkness closed around him. With hands outstretched, he groped forward, wondering if the nun was planning some kind of ambush.

He bumped into a metal wall, made what felt like a half turn to the left and kept on going. The next bend in the duct brought him out into the light again.

The nun hadn't bothered to replace the outside grating. As soon as Christopher stepped through, he realized he was a full studio street away from the ladies' room.

Squinting against the rain, he swiveled his head. The street was empty. There was no sign of the nun, or anyone else for that matter.

Christopher grimaced as water dripped from his halo, landing on his nose and splashing into his eyes. He lowered his head to blink and that's when he saw the first of the waterlogged hundred-dollar bills.

A few yards further on he found another sodden banknote. Either the nun had been careless, or the driving rain had disintegrated the paper bag. The thought of all that loot scattered to hell and gone renewed Christopher. At a jog, he followed the trail as far as the props department, where the money ran out.

15

STILL DRESSED AS an angel, but with his earthly clothes draped over one arm, Christopher went looking for Bill Bowzer. But the game show offices were totally deserted, without so much as a secretary to harass him. Only then did the reporter realize the reason; "Wheeler-Dealers" was only moments away from taping. And for that daily ceremony Bowzer required all hands on deck, just in case he drew an audience reluctant to applaud his brilliance.

Feeling quite dull himself, Christopher shivered inside his heavenly gown, then hurried across the suite, down the hall and into Bowzer's private retreat. As soon as the angel's garb had been stripped away, the reporter retrieved his own clothes from their plastic carrier.

Sporting goose bumps head to toe, he went looking for a towel in Bowzer's star-sized bathroom. Once dry and dressed, the reporter felt comfortable for the first time all day. But when he stared out at the unending rain, depression as gray as the day settled over him.

The thought of going out again sent him reeling toward one of two massive couches. There, he collapsed. A sigh escaped him as he began to relax. That was more like it. All he needed now was a good book to take his mind off things.

He lurched back onto his feet and stepped behind Bowzer's desk to get at the bookcase. A leather-bound set of Charles Dickens caught his eye. But when he reached for *Great Expectations*, the book wouldn't budge. In that instant he realized that only the spines were real; they'd been glued on a facade. Bowzer's library was a prop.

Idly, he wondered if the panel had been built especially for the MC or if it had been salvaged from some previous ABN production.

Without hope of finding a complete book, Christopher began tugging at titles of interest. Finally a yank on Anthony Trollope revealed that the library was on a hinge. It swung open to disclose real shelves inside. Only they didn't hold books. They held row upon row of video tapes, judging by the titles, a connoisseur's collection of pornography.

To make certain of his diagnosis, Christopher decided to sample at random. Extracting "Whips of Pleasure" from the middle of a shelf, he loaded the cassette into Bowzer's tape machine, then warmed up the giant-screen TV.

But before Christopher could push the start button, Bowzer himself burst into the room. "Someone saw you sneaking around in my office."

"Aren't you supposed to be taping?"

"Don't change the subject."

"I came here to change my clothes."

Bowzer glared at the angel's sopping remains. Then he seemed to hold his breath until his eyes bulged. Finally a shout erupted from his quivering lips. "You have no respect for property."

"So all this *is* yours."

Only then did Bowzer realize that his library was unhinged. "You bastard. Get out!"

Christopher's response was to start the video tape. Despite the title, "Whips of Pleasure" didn't look all that pleasant to him. "Is this part of God's work, Bowzer?"

With each crack of the whip, the game show host winced.

"What would your fans say?"

"For Godsake, man, I pay my dues. Twenty hours of charity work a week. Every year I entertain at Children's Hospital."

Christopher waved at the sixty-inch screen. "After seeing this no mother would let you anywhere near her children."

"What do you want from me?" Bowzer asked, a plea.

"How about the truth?"

"How much? Just tell me."

"Only the truth."

Bowzer's eyes went wide with disbelief.

"You don't have any choice," the reporter added as he switched off the pornography. "Do you have anything starring Al Aarons?"

Bowzer's eyes narrowed. "Now I get it. This is some kind of news coverup."

"Just answer my question. Did Bingo sell you the Aarons tape?"

"If Al's an X-rated star, I never saw him."

"Then what was Bingo doing here earlier?"

"Okay, so I lied to you before. I've been buying from him for years. Most of these tapes came from him. Hellsakes, a man in my position can't afford to deal in public, you know. I'd be recognized anywhere. My face is better known than most movie stars. So I've had to use Bingo as my middleman."

One of Bowzer's nubile production assistants knocked at the open door. "The audience is getting restless, Bill."

"I'll be right there."

"The director says the crew's going on overtime."

Bowzer looked to Christopher for guidance.

The reporter said, "You go ahead, Bill, I've got a few things to clean up around here. And remember, I know I can count on your discretion. After all, you can't reveal news secrets without exposing yourself."

It was an unhappy looking MC who followed his production assistant from the office. As soon as they were gone, Christopher picked up the phone and called the technical building. He got the shift supervisor, Fat Jack Pollard, on the line.

"I have some tapes that need erasing," the reporter explained.

"Have you been hoarding again?"

"I'm going to make your day, Jack. There are hundreds of them here."

"Where are you?"

Christopher told him.

"I'll send a man right over to pick them up."

16

CHRISTOPHER BEGAN THE day feeling sorry for himself. "And with good reason," he grumbled. First, he'd let the nun get away. On top of that, Susan hadn't spoken to him since learning about the rabies shots. And finally, TV was weighing on him like Jacob Marley's chain. To shed it, he would have to find an alternative lifestyle.

He tore the month of April from his kitchen calendar, intending to use the back to make a list of likely professions. But none came to mind.

With a groan, he dumped April to rummage through a pile of old newspapers. After a while, he came up with last Sunday's classified ads. There, literally hundreds of occupations were listed. But he didn't seem qualified for any of them.

"Face it," he muttered, "without the tube you'd be out of work."

The thought sent him into the garage to feed his family of raccoons, which he'd acquired after discovering that his original catch had been a female. The possibility of her family starving to death had sent him out into the night in search of humane traps and tasty bait.

It had taken him hours crawling on a wet roof and in a musty attic to snare all five. Since then his garage had smelled like the zoo on a hot day.

"How about a little cat food and kibble?" he asked. "Just like the health department ordered."

They growled from their hiding place behind the garbage cans.

"Yeah, I know how you feel. Junk food tastes a lot better."

As soon as he returned to the doorway they came out to eat, with gusto.

"This is a fine mess," he went on. "A two-week quarantine in my garage. I tried to get the county to take you, but they claimed to be fresh out of cage space."

Their only answer was to lick their bowls.

"Those traps cost me a fortune."

The stink had Christopher breathing through his mouth. He closed the door but the aroma lingered on, reminding him of the stink at Channel 3, where something smelled far worse than raccoon droppings. But no one seemed to want to do anything about it. No one but him.

The raccoon smell stayed with him, probably on the soles of his shoes, all the way to the freeway. His Mustang, which often smelled like manure when its catalytic converter acted up, bucked and coughed as water from the roadway did its best to drown the beast.

Irma had lived in Highland Park. There, the surface streets were like shallow rivers. Fording them could only be done at a crawl.

When he rolled down the car window in an attempt to read house numbers, a miracle happened. The rain stopped.

Through a break in the clouds, sunlight dazzled him. For a moment all he could see was afterburn. He braked the Mustang to a stop and waited for sight to return. When it did, the neighborhood looked worse than ever. Cars were parked everywhere: along the curb, in driveways, on soggy front lawns. Many stood high off the ground, resting on huge white-lettered tires. By comparison to the vehicles on display, the houses looked shabby.

Christopher had no choice but to pull his Mustang onto Irma's overgrown yard. The house, peeling gray stucco with a green tarpaper roof, was the runt of the area. Its front door stood wide open, probably left that way by vandals.

Several children suddenly appeared, drawn either by the sun or the reporter's arrival. A couple of them stopped to watch Christopher shyly, while the others ran in through Irma's front door. He followed. Seeing him in pursuit, they fled down a hallway. A moment later a screen door slammed. Then the house was silent.

Christopher wrinkled his nose. For a moment he thought he'd tracked in the smell. Then he realized that the aroma of dogs pervaded everything, though none were to be seen. But they'd left evidence of their occupancy behind. Hair matted each piece of threadbare furniture.

On the walls pictures of St. Christopher hung everywhere. None of them had been defaced. For that matter, there was no sign of vandalism anywhere.

The reporter heard a noise behind him and sprang around in time to meet two youngsters head-on. The older one, a boy of about ten, bounced off and kept right on going, while the younger child, a girl, tripped and fell. She immediately began to cry.

Christopher knelt to comfort her.

She sobbed. "If you touch me, I'll yell rape."

Did she know what she was saying? he wondered. Or was that something she'd been told to tell strangers?

"I'm a friend of Irma's," he said softly.

The girl, no more than seven or eight, knuckled her brown eyes. "Are you going to get her dogs back?"

"What happened to them?"

The child shook her head.

"I'm here to help," he assured her.

She didn't respond.

"Do you know where Irma is?" he asked.

"Oh, yes." The girl nodded emphatically. "She's in the cemetery."

The sun disappeared behind clouds, turning the room dark and cold. The girl hugged herself.

Christopher didn't know what to say. He was about to stand up when the child pointed to the pictures on the wall. "St. Christopher watches over little children. Irma said so."

"I didn't know that."

"Oh, yes. Little children and animals. If you look at the pictures, you can see him doing it." The girl got to her feet, took Christopher's hand, and led him in a circle around the room. "Watch St. Christopher's eyes," she told him solemnly. "They follow you wherever you go."

Christopher nodded.

"Irma said so," the little girl added as if proving her case.

"Let my sister go," a boy said from the doorway. It was the boy who had bounced off Christopher.

"*I'm* holding *him*," the girl said, taking her hand away.

"I have a big brother," the boy threatened.

Christopher raised his hands in surrender.

Eyes wide with disbelief at capturing an adult, the youngster shaped his fingers into a gun to keep his prisoner covered.

"He won't shoot," the girl said. To her brother she added, "He's a friend of Irma's."

A skeptical squint puckered the boy's face. Either that or he was taking aim. "No one ever came to see her. That's why she let us play in her house, because she was lonesome." He flexed his thumb as if getting ready to fire. "If you were such a good friend, how come we never saw you before?"

The little girl looked up at Christopher for an explanation.

He didn't need any more guilt than he already had. "I work at Channel 3. That's where I met Irma." He opened his raincoat and pointed to the gold "3" on his lapel.

"Is your name Christopher?" the boy asked.

"That's right."

"Irma talked a lot about you. She was always watching your news. She said you were named for St. Christopher."

The reporter spread his hands.

"I don't believe it either," the boy said. "Old Irma was crazy."

"Was not," his sister countered.

"Was too."

107

"Not."

"Everybody says so."

"Who?" Christopher asked.

The boy looked smug. "Dad."

"He never did," the girl said.

Her brother nodded to the contrary. "She was strange."

Lowering his arms, Christopher strained to catch every nuance. The boy, reflecting his elders, might provide the only clear portrait available. Certainly his father wouldn't be likely to repeat such things to a stranger, especially a reporter.

"She never locked her doors for one thing. And she liked the racket and mess us kids made."

"Irma sounds like a nice lady to me," Christopher offered.

The boy, tired of pointing his fingers, shoved both hands into his jeans, then hung his head. Obviously he had liked Irma too but didn't know how to admit it. "She took in all the dogs and cats that came around. She had dozens of them." He peered around the room. "Jerry was my favorite. He was a black cat."

His sister interjected that she preferred a more recent acquisition, a puppy named Ted.

Her brother continued. "They were eating her out of house and home, my dad said. He says that about us too." He went to his sister and took her hand.

"Irma always made us cookies," she said. "She even baked snacks for her animals."

With one hand the boy rubbed his eyes. "She had one of those metal shopping carts. She kept it for sick animals, so she could wheel them to the vet's down the street."

The reporter scanned the room again, half expecting to see St. Francis up there among all the Christophers.

The boy's eyes glistened on the verge of tears. "All her hard work was for nothing." He blinked. It wasn't his father he was repeating now. "As soon as Irma died, someone called the pound to come and take away her pets."

★ ★ ★

Christopher had to wait his turn at the veterinarian's. Ahead of him was a black and white bull terrier, which kept showing incredibly large teeth.

"Katie's friendly," the dog's owner said.

The terrier's beady black eyes said otherwise.

Christopher moved to the other side of the waiting room, where he sat with his feet in a puddle that was definitely not rain.

The terrier trembled when its turn came and had to be dragged into the examination room, trailing a fresh stream, which became a tributary to Christopher's puddle.

Growls came through the closed door. Christopher struck "veterinarian" off his list of potential occupations.

When the reporter finally got in to see the doctor, the man seemed ill at ease and kept staring at Christopher's feet as if hoping to find an animal there he was familiar with.

The reporter explained the reason for his visit.

"I didn't know Irma was dead."

"I'm trying to find out who killed her."

"And her animals?"

"Apparently the city took them away."

The vet sighed. "I told her she was in violation of the law. Anything over three animals and you're classified as a kennel. She was out of zone for that."

"Tell me about her."

The man studied the Channel 3 emblem for a moment. "She was a character, that's for sure." The vet ran a hand through his hair, which was as curly as a spaniel's ear. "She used to bring in stray animals and expect me to work on them free of charge." He smiled at the memory. "And you know what? I did too. But finally I had to put a stop to that. It got so she had enough animals to keep the entire clinic busy."

"That's when you stopped seeing her, I take it?"

"Not at all. She kept right on bringing them in."

"I don't understand."

"She came into money. At least, that's what she said.

109

She told me that for once in her life she could afford to have as many pets as she wanted. It's a wonder the city didn't get after her sooner."

Christopher took a deep breath. "What about the money?"

"It's funny now that I think about it. She said it was dirty money, but that spending it on animals made it clean."

"Did she say why it was dirty?"

"I never thought to ask her. Since it was Irma speaking, I didn't think that much about it at the time."

Christopher sighed. "Her patron ought to have been St. Francis."

"I see you know about her and St. Christopher."

Without warning, the vet banged the heel of his hand against his forehead like a man who'd suddenly seen the light. "I thought I recognized you. The last time Irma was in here she mentioned you. Called you her saint's namesake."

Christopher closed his eyes and breathed deeply, but he couldn't dispel his ever growing guilt.

"I called her our local St. Francis once," the vet went on. "And you know what her answer was?"

The man paused until Christopher shook his head.

"She told me that she didn't believe in owning animals. That they were only traveling through this life on their way to someplace better, the same way people are."

The vet's face wrinkled at the memory. "She said that's why all of us need the patron saint of travelers."

Wind-whipped rain stung Christopher all the way to the Mustang. Even inside the car he wasn't safe from attack. Water had breached the windshield seal and was spraying him in the face. The earlier moment of sunshine seemed like a hallucination.

After a couple of miles, the leaking water had doubled the weight of his corduroy sportscoat. But it was nothing compared to the burden of his conscience, which had developed a gravity all its own. Soon he wouldn't be able to move under the weight of it. But then, he deserved such a fate for succumbing to Reisner the night Irma had sought help. Three-second inserts with Christopher spewing, "Film at eleven" had come before an old lady who needed saving.

One look at her should have told him that she was in love with small children and animals. Yet he had been blind to her in the beginning, seeing only one of those mothlike lunatics attracted to the deadly light of television.

Today, even rain failed to dampen TV's deadly attraction. Pickets milled around ABN's front gate, sign wavers who wanted to see themselves on the news, or would-be stars hoping to be discovered. One of them, a scrawny woman pushing a shopping cart filled with soggy paper bags, reminded Christopher of Irma. He was tempted to stop and talk until he saw her picket sign. WHEELER-DEALERS UNITE.

"Wheeler-Dealers" wanted a free ride, while Irma had offered to pay for Christopher's help.

What was it she had said? That she could afford to pay him because she was getting a regular bonus from the station. Was that the same as the dirty money she'd told the veterinarian about? And what was the mortal sin she'd half confessed to Father John?

Christopher stopped the car and backed up, deciding to bypass the main gate in favor of the employee parking entrance, which didn't have the glamour to attract pickets.

The reporter's parking place, the one with his name on it, already held a car, Gossett's. Christopher shouted a curse before moving on. But not a space was to be found. His only option now was to park illegally, a major offense at ABN. Paying the fine wasn't so bad, but listening to the lecture that went along with it was pure torture. In the event that Christopher suffered such a fate, he promised Gossett a flat tire. Two flat tires.

The reporter maneuvered down a narrow street between the shop area and the props department and entered the never-never land of executive parking. But even there, he was out of luck. All network vice presidents were present and accounted for.

The street between the news building and stage B had a red stripe down the middle, indicating no parking on either side. But Christopher brought the Mustang to a stop anyway. Maybe they'd tow the damned thing away and he could claim it as stolen.

Switching off the ignition, he sat there cursing Gossett and wiping rain water from his face. After a moment, Gossett faded. Irma returned. Could her dirty money have come from pornography?

Christopher took a deep breath, then expelled it toward the windshield, which immediately fogged. Perfect, he thought. Just like his foresight. Or was that hindsight? He shrugged. Both were fogged.

Whatever the case, he was going to have to renew his attack. His main objective would be Bingo Bradford. And if that didn't work out, there was always the porno star himself, Al Aarons. But first he had to see Susan.

17

A COMPANY OF soaking wet GI's surrounded Christopher the moment he stepped from his car. They carried him along like a prisoner of war.

"Civilian," someone muttered, making it sound like a curse.

Their M 1 rifles intimidated him.

"You'd think they could wait for a sunny day," a sergeant said to him as if Christopher had suddenly become a representative of the network.

"It was easier to rewrite the script," a platoon leader responded, "than hold up the shooting."

Christopher knew exactly how the "Battleguard" extras felt. For years Herb Reisner had been rewriting the reporter's life. First, the news director had made him an action reporter, then a consumer advocate. The title changed depending upon what the ratings needed.

He escaped the GI's ranks only to be caught up by a contingent of SS. Both sides were on their way to war on the back lot.

But Christopher had his own battle to fight. He scrambled free of the troops and ran for Stage C, his back itching as he thought how easy it would be to replace a blank with a real bullet in one of those M1's.

"Emergency Hospital" had sprung a leak. Plastic tarps were everywhere, flung over the nursing station, draped around the operating table, even masking the bank of cardboard elevators. The floor itself was awash with water, and the mopping propmen couldn't keep up with the flow. Over the studio loudspeaker the director wanted to know if anyone had heard from the roofers.

There were conflicting responses from half a dozen staf-

113

fers on stage. Finally an associate director suggested that props use plastic tarps on the roof. That, however, required a ruling on union jurisdictions. The cry went up for Kraut Wagner, the shop steward.

Without waiting to see how negotiations went, Christopher dripped all the way to Susan's dressing room. His knock produced an angry, "Come in." While the door was still opening, she added, "My hair looks awful."

Christopher waved a white handkerchief across the threshold.

"So it's you!" She sounded even more annoyed.

"Good news."

"You're being traded to another channel."

"Better than that. I caught all the raccoons. With any luck, you won't have to be taking those shots."

"Unless they start foaming at the mouth," she reminded him.

"They look healthy."

"So did Jack the Ripper."

"Susan, what else do you want me to do?"

She turned back to her mirror. "Do you know anything about hair dressing?"

"You look beautiful just as you are." She wore a filmy negligee, as revealing as Broadcast Standards would allow.

"Who's your TV lover today?" he asked.

The anger began fading from her face. He grinned at her. For a moment she tried not to respond. But it was a losing battle. Finally she laughed and offered her cheek to be kissed.

He gave her a quick peck. Even that brief touch seemed electric. The smell of her forced him to clasp his hands behind his back to keep from exploring the negligee.

"How long will they have to be in quarantine?" she asked.

"Two weeks."

"It ought to be safe in your bed for another fourteen days then."

"I'll nail up the roof as soon as I get home."

She stood up and moved close to him. "Well?"

He kissed her lightly on the lips.

Her mouth went to work as if she were trying to gobble him up. It was like a male fantasy come true. Only now Christopher wasn't responding. Irma had ruined his sex drive, because what he wanted to do first was ask questions.

"What's wrong?" Susan asked after a moment.

"Someone might come in."

"There's a lock on the door."

Christopher made no move to fasten it.

"All right. I know that look of yours. You're playing front-page reporter."

"It's not a role I'm playing."

Susan touched his cheek gently. "I know." Then she sat at her dressing table, picked up the phone and called for makeup.

A moment later a short, middle-aged woman appeared and began to work on Susan's hair.

Christopher started to leave, but the actress called him back. "If you've got something you want to ask me, go ahead. Don't mind Millie here."

Millie glanced at Christopher in the mirror. Her expressionless face said she was used to being part of the furniture.

For a moment, he tried to think of a way around what he wanted to ask. But in the end he said, "You were seen sitting in the ambulance with Mark Lambert on the day of the killings."

"He's being buried today," Susan said.

"That's quick."

"Don't be silly. On the show. The writers worked all night to figure a way to get rid of one lover and find me another. Wait till you see it. It's really ingenius."

Millie finished with Susan's hair and began applying makeup.

"What about the ambulance?"

"Who saw me?"

Christopher didn't consider Kraut Wagner a source worth protecting. But the reporter kept the propman anonymous just the same. "I did."

"Now, I suppose you're jealous."

Millie's fingers hesitated for an instant, then went on applying makeup to Susan's long neck. Christopher watched in fascination as the makeup pad moved down into the low-cut negligee.

"I just want to know what happened," he said, meeting Susan's taunting eyes in the mirror over her makeup table.

Her brow wrinkled. The expression prompted a quick tap of rebuke on her forehead from Millie. To keep from cracking her makeup, Susan spoke through clenched teeth like a ventriloquist, a bad one. "Mark came to me for help."

For a moment, Christopher didn't understand what she'd said, didn't realize that she'd left out the M's to keep from wrinkling her face while makeup was being applied.

"He'd been on this show two years," Susan continued, still trying not to put creases in her face, "longer than anyone else except Jason. In all that time, he never had a raise."

On a soap, Christopher recalled, AFTRA union minimum called for nearly four thousand a week.

"He was going in to demand a raise from the executive producer."

"So why did he need your help?"

"Mark figured he could succeed only if we both went in together. Otherwise, they'd just write him out of the script. Hell, it's been done before. Every two years for that matter, because that's when the AFTRA minimum takes a two thousand a week jump. Management would rather create a new character than pay that."

Millie thumped Susan again. After that, the actress remained silent until the makeup woman left the dressing room. "He figured they couldn't write us both out. But I knew better. Nothing would be easier than to kill us in a car crash. Off camera and out of work. Our fans would never see us again. When I die on this show, I want to go on camera, milking it for every damn tear I can get."

"So you told him no."

"I wished him luck of course. If somehow he managed to get more money, I could probably do the same. You realize, of course, that I've just given upper management the perfect motive for murder—the bottom line. It kills more careers than anything else."

Christopher added actor to the growing list of professions that didn't suit him.

"What about Ed Flemming?" he asked. "Why was he in on that conversation in the ambulance?"

"I . . ." She tilted her head suddenly, studying Christopher. Her sigh, when it came, was slow and deliberate. "I knew it. You're playing detective."

"Look, Susan, I—"

"Don't look so grim. It's all right. I'll go along and answer your questions."

He started to say something but she stopped him with a gesture. "Mark and Flemming were close friends. I mean *close*. So it was no wonder he wanted Flemming's advice."

"What do you mean by close?"

"Exactly what you think."

"Could you be mistaken about them?"

If her assessment of Flemming was correct, his office couch had never seen the likes of Susan.

She wrinkled her brow, then realized what she'd done and peered anxiously into the mirror to appraise damage. Seeing no telltale cracks, she wet her lips and said, "That's the impression I got."

Christopher still had trouble believing it. An ambitious man like Flemming couldn't afford male friendships. While such flings might be acceptable among actors, at the executive level in the television industry they could kill a career faster than Arab money. He said as much to Susan.

"I don't know anything about the man's ambitions,"

she said. "Sure, he liked to hang around the set keeping his eye on Mark. But that's all. That's practically the only time I ever saw him."

"Maybe he was keeping his eyes on you?"

Susan shrugged, a gesture that did wonderful things to the clinging negligee. "I never considered that for a moment."

"Why not?"

"If you're a woman you can tell when a man is interested. Now *you*, I can read like a book. As for Flemming, I never paid that much attention to him. After all, he's only the local sales manager, and 'Emergency Hospital' is strictly network."

"Flemming says otherwise."

"About what?"

"He says you do favors for him."

"I don't like what you're implying."

"Do you go out with Flemming's clients or not?"

"Never."

As a reporter Christopher had learned to read people. He usually got a sinking sensation in his gut when he was being lied to. But that didn't work with Susan, because he got that same feeling every time he looked at her.

"Why were you lying down in the back of the ambulance?" he blurted out before he could lose his nerve.

Her answering smile made him feel like a guilty child. "Come on. I'll show you."

She took his hands, her nails playing games in his palm. The contact threatened his equilibrium. Then she led him toward large sliding doors at the rear of the studio. There, an ambulance had been backed halfway up a ramp that led to the soundstage.

"A rental," she explained. "The police still have our regular one." She opened the back door to reveal a wall-to-wall air mattress on the floor inside.

"Shall we?" With that, she started to crawl onto the mattress. When Christopher held back she said, "Just be careful of my hair, that's all." She patted the bedding next to her.

He eased inside.

"You see?" she said, closing the door behind him. "I was just looking for a nice place for us to meet." She kissed him, her hands roaming freely. "I wouldn't do something like this with Ed Flemming."

From the front end of the vehicle, which protruded beyond the building's overhang, came the roar of pounding rain. With one eye, Christopher managed to check the windshield. The glass might as well have been painted over. No one could see in through that kind of deluge.

Even so, he pulled back from her lips.

"Don't worry about my makeup," she murmured. "Millie can do it again."

"The stage hands," he said into her ravenous mouth.

"They'll just think we're rehearsing," she answered.

But for Christopher it was the real thing.

Hatless, without even an umbrella, Christopher ran in the rain. His soggy pantlegs, his squishing shoes, all felt suddenly weightless. Even the plastic raincoat, which was steaming him like a clam, made delightful flapping noises as he ran. He was jubilant; he was in love.

Now all he had to do was free his conscience of Irma and he'd be a completely happy man. To that end, he ran all the way to the technical building in search of Bingo Bradford. But there, in answer to a simple question, Fat Jack Pollard turned red and shouted, "That bastard! He didn't show up for work today. I had to bring someone in on golden time to cover for him."

"What about his house?"

"I already called there. No answer."

"Does he do this often?"

"Never when it's time for his bingo game. That's what's got me stymied." The shift supervisor rubbed the small of his back against the edge of the doorframe. "The last time I saw him yesterday, he was on his way to props, or so he said."

Christopher started to leave.

"If you find him," Fat Jack called after the reporter, "tell the bastard this is one time I'm not punching him in."

The props department was deserted. No doubt Kraut Wagner had called out all his boys to cope with Stage C's leaking roof. That left Christopher with a decision. He opted for flaunting all sorts of union prohibitions and went searching on his own, remembering that the blackmailer had trailed money in the direction of Props.

Moving stealthily, the reporter began wandering through a bizarre landscape of old sets. Almost immediately, he found himself in a mock newsroom, all that remained of a short-lived rip-off of "The Mary Tyler Moore Show." Too bad anchormen really weren't like Ted Baxter, afraid of producers and news directors. In real life, the Ted Baxters of this world were vicious and went by the name of Al Aarons.

A wave of nostalgia swept Christopher into "The Night Zone," another ABN rip-off. This time the target had been "The Twilight Zone." Strangely enough, the ABN show had been moderately successful after a lawsuit which necessitated a title change to "Night Creatures." It's reruns were still to be found on Channel 3 on Sunday afternoons.

Christopher fought his way through phony cobwebs, which had acquired real spiders, and was still frantically brushing himself as he reached "The New Adventures of Sherlock Holmes."

Give it up, he told himself. Bingo wasn't the kind of man to hide in the past. Besides, there might be something worse than spiders inhabiting the derelict sets.

Certainly 221B Baker Street had seen better days. Even in the dim light from the naked bulbs hanging overhead, Christopher could see a couple of small holes in the wall.

He was about to poke a finger through one when he stepped in something sticky.

He held his breath and prayed that he was mistaken, that a rain leak had somehow turned the color of blood.

Aware that he was leaving gory footprints, the reporter moved quietly around the wall. On the other side, he found more blood but no body, a discovery that brought a sigh of relief. Perhaps rain had mixed with something nasty on the roof before leaking inside.

All at once Christopher realized that he'd been holding his breath. And just as suddenly, he was feeling so shaky he needed to sit down. Sherlock Holmes's hansom cab caught his eye.

"Come, Watson," he managed to gasp, "the game is afoot."

The cab, however, was taken. But its occupant wasn't going anywhere.

Christopher fought his gag reflex all the way back to Kraut Wagner's office. There, he made two quick calls, one to the news room, the other to the executive bungalow. Only then did he use an outside line to notify the police of the death of Bingo Bradford, still in nun's costume.

The holes in 221B Baker Street had been bullet holes, two of them. There were also two holes in Bingo. This time no one could call it suicide.

18

"THE POLICE ARE calling it suicide!" Christopher bellowed.

"Calm down," Herb Reisner said quietly, "and tell me what happened."

Squinting at the plaque over the news director's desk, Christopher thought mean. "I talked to them for hours, those two detectives. Just when I felt they were finally beginning to believe me, Mike Baker shows up waving his public relations banner. The moment he hears they found a gun in Bingo's hand, he starts talking murder-suicide again. Another killer filled with remorse, Baker says. Bingo must have driven the ambulance, must have killed Lambert, and then done himself in. It doesn't bother Baker one bit that Bingo shot himself twice. Or that Lambert was a suicide in the last scenario. When I pointed that out, he says either way, Lambert or Bingo, one or the other is a suicide, and now everything's tidy. Remorse, says Baker, has seen justice done. Bullshit, says I, letting it slip that the nun had been committing blackmail."

"Oh, God."

"Of course, I told them the nun outfit doesn't mean a thing without the money. And there was no money to be found. So that definitely makes it murder. I told them that in no uncertain terms."

"And what did they say?" Reisner asked.

"They're waiting for the autopsy."

"There you go then. LAPD isn't about to sweep murder under the rug, you know that. Besides, someone else may have found the money before you got there. Finders, keepers. Twenty-five thousand is enough to corrupt most people."

"That's not the point."

"Just what the hell are you yelling about then?" The news director's bad eye, the one that got out of whack under pressure, shimmied momentarily.

"I know Irma O'Donnell is at the center of everything that's happened. But nobody wants to believe it."

Reisner snorted. "A porno ring I might buy. Maybe even one of Bingo's disgruntled customers turned maniac. But a cleaning lady Mafia? Come on, Bobbo."

Christopher glared at the news director until the man's eye wobbled. After that, the reporter transferred his gaze to the sign on the wall. Even with his eyes closed, he could read "Think Mean" in afterburn.

When he no longer saw writing on his eyelids, he said, "I need your help, Herb."

The news director immediately swiveled his executive chair out of Christopher's line of sight. "Now I know you're desperate."

"It will be good for the ratings."

Reisner's chair came halfway around toward the reporter.

"At a million dollars a point, you'll be able to retire on what I have in mind."

The chair returned to its original position, but Reisner kept his eyes averted, as if reading additional plaques of wisdom on the ceiling.

"Live and in color, I'm going to smoke out Irma's killer."

"And just how do you intend to do that?" The news director's eyes came down to earth totally out of control. He buried his head in his hands. "I'm waiting."

"I think I know a few of the answers now," Christopher said. "I just need a way to make use of the information."

"Have you told the police what you want to do?"

"If they won't buy Irma, what chance do I have selling them either my theories or my plan?"

"So you're selling me instead?"

"I need a platform."

"My 'Six O'Clock News.'"

"Exactly."

123

"Who do you have to slander?"

"The only person you'll have to worry about is me. By making a few guesses on the air, guesses that sound like I know a lot more than I'm telling, I'll set myself up as a target."

"Can you guarantee that you'll be shot on camera?"

"Just think of the ratings, Herb."

The news director groaned. "Let me hear some of those guesses of yours."

"It's no secret on this lot that Bingo pirated anything, not just pornography. If you wanted one of the new movies, all you had to do was slip Bingo enough money. As for his X-rated customers, you'd be surprised at the famous names on his list."

"Who?"

"You don't want slander on 'The Six O'Clock News.' "

"I don't think I want you either."

Ignoring the comment, Christopher continued. "Unless I miss my guess, our Bingo was in the position to blackmail a lot of people on this lot, not just Al Aarons."

"Can you prove all this?"

"I don't have to. All I have to do is convince someone that I'm dangerous enough to kill. And all you have to do is remember that I don't intend to commit suicide, no matter what Mike Baker might tell you. Besides, I found the chicken suit in props. It was still wet."

Reisner groaned.

"When the cops asked Kraut about it, he admitted making a rental deal with Bingo for costumes. But Kraut swears that Bingo never dressed as a surgeon, only as a nun and a bird."

"Wait a minute." The news director straightened up and blinked. "If Aarons found out about that, that would make him the number one suspect." He slipped a palm over his left eye and pressed so hard muscles in his arm quivered.

"That would be too much to hope for," Christopher said.

Reisner freed his eye. "Maybe Bingo did kill himself after all. Or maybe he was murdered for the twenty-five thousand. Either way, that would let AA off the hook. He wouldn't have the guts to kill for money."

"I hope the police believe him."

"I still might end up in Pocatello for obstructing justice."

"Brewster's already sweet-talked the detectives."

"*Him*, I hope they believe."

"They're willing to overlook us keeping blackmail from them."

"Thank God."

"I just wish Brewster had gone further and told them that Lambert was a smoke screen, a way of putting an end to any further investigation. Or that Bingo, too, was a diversion in his own way, a means of turning murder into suicide a second time if the first one wasn't believed."

"You make your killer sound like a genius."

"Nothing else makes any sense."

"You've been watching too much television. In real life things aren't supposed to make sense."

"So you do agree with me."

"No. You still haven't convinced me that the old girl is the center of things."

"Herb, I can't prove it. I can't even account for it. But I know it inside. I can feel it."

"I don't put feelings on the air. They're too dangerous."

19

THE PITIFUL SOUNDS coming from the garage ruined Christopher's appetite, something of an achievement. He abandoned a piece of carrot cake and peeked through the connecting door from the kitchen to see what all the howling was about.

Their food bowls were empty.

"Only thirteen days to go," he told them, while carefully edging into the garage to pour out more kibble.

The sound of his voice triggered pathetic mewing from the young raccoons. "I know you want your freedom. But I can't let you go."

If he did, Susan would have to undergo rabies shots.

He sighed, then kept right on breathing through his mouth to avoid the stench. What he needed was a dog run so they could get exercise and fresh air. Maybe he could have a chain-link enclosure built in the backyard. He was about to go check the yellow pages for fence companies when he realized that any kind of adequate construction would be impossible in such weather.

Once back in the house he heard the sound of happy grunts as the raccoons attacked the food. But after a while he detected a different kind of sound, a sort of chomping. There was no telling what they might be chewing on, anything from his old ten-speed to electrical wiring.

To hell with it, he decided. He'd let the smoke detector in the garage do the worrying. Meanwhile, he needed sleep. A good night's sleep.

In the bedroom, he checked the ceiling. Water had stopped coming down, but what remained of the plaster looked unstable. Besides that, his soggy mattress still smelled like mating raccoons.

With a defeated shrug, he slouched into the living room, kicked off his shoes, and sat on the sofa, a piece of furniture that denied comfort in any position. After a moment's hesitation, he switched off the table lamp on the end table and stretched out. Lumps and cushion ridges immediately began torturing his back. He rolled over and removed his wallet, fat with plastic lifelines to Visa and Master Charge.

"A good night's sleep," he reminded himself and immediately remembered that he hadn't set the alarm clock. With a grunt, he got up and shuffled back into the bedroom, retrieved the clock, set it for ten-fifteen, two hours from now, then carried it back to the sofa.

"Two hours is better than nothing," he said without conviction, then forced his eyes closed and listened to rain pounding on the roof. And that made him wonder if his patched shingles would hold until better weather. So far, it had been raining for seven days straight. Throughout Southern California, Jonahs calling themselves Noahs were predicting the worst. No doubt Wayne Gossett was still at his desk, glorying in overtime and disaster damage. When there were victims to be videotaped, nothing could budge the assignment editor from his police and fire radios.

Stop it, Christopher told himself. Forget Gossett. Forget Channel 3 for a while.

By the time Christopher arrived at Channel 3, the news studio was just coming to life. It was 10:45, fifteen minutes away from the late news.

In the small makeup room just off the set, he found Al Aarons studying himself in the full-length mirror. Every strand of the anchorman's carefully woven toupee was in place. There was no telltale stripe around his collar where tan makeup left off and pale flesh began.

Leaning up against the glass, Aarons used trembling fingers to spread wide his eyelids.

"On camera," he muttered, "your eyes are everything. It's these baby blues that hook your audience, Christopher, keep them from changing channels. Without eyes like this, an anchorman's nothing. Of course, key lights don't hurt."

"Ten minutes to air," a voice announced over the loudspeakers on stage.

Aarons stuck out his tongue, then examined it with a finger. "It's a wonder I can go on at all, what with blackmail and dead men everywhere."

He made a sad face, the one he reserved for reading disasters on the air. Then his lips pressed into a fine, condemning line. But the grim expression lasted only a moment before a chuckle spilled out. "I've got to hand it to you, Christopher. You did a good job plucking that chicken for me."

"I had nothing to do with it."

Still peering into the mirror, AA stepped back to get a full view of himself. His blue blazer and tie were perfect. Below the waist, where the camera never reached, he wore cut-off jeans and old tennis shoes. Once, on a bet, he'd done the news naked from the waist down.

"Whoever it was did me a favor killing that chicken."

"We're talking about a man. Bingo Bradford."

AA shrugged.

Lunging out, Christopher grabbed hold of Aarons's toupee. The anchorman opened his mouth to scream.

"One word," the reporter cautioned, "and I'll rip it off."

Aarons went absolutely still. The woven mixture of real and synthetic hair was an artistic masterpiece. One sudden jerk and he would be off the air for a day at least. Maybe more. As it was, it took the hairdresser hours each week to keep Aarons looking like he did.

"You're crazy," the anchorman said. "You . . . you're in with that chicken."

Aarons went up on tiptoe to compensate for steadily increasing pressure on his toupee. Christopher leaned close and whispered, "Do you know what happens to anchormen who don't go on the air during Sweeps?"

Aarons swallowed noisily, not saying a word.

"They disappear forever, that's what."

"You . . ." AA paused to wet his lips. "I'll have you fired for this."

With his free hand, Christopher closed the dressing room door. "I don't see any witnesses."

The five-minute warning sounded, muffled but quite understandable.

"What do you want?" Aarons asked, his tone turning to surrender.

"I'm interested in your movies," Christopher said into the anchorman's ear.

"There's not much time."

"Don't waste it then."

"What do you want to know?"

"Start talking. I'll let you know when I hear it."

Aarons spoke rapidly. "I've been trying to buy up prints of that movie for years. I hadn't seen or heard of any for a long time, not until that chicken showed up. I realize now, of course, it was Bingo Bradford."

"That gives you the perfect motive for murder."

"I had no idea who the chicken was, not until the police questioned me this evening. At first, I didn't make the connection with the nun's costume. But then they told me a chicken disguise had been found nearby. They already knew about the blackmail."

Christopher's fingers tightened on the toupee.

"What do you want?" Aarons's voice squeaked. "Just tell me."

"What do you know about Irma O'Donnell?"

"Nothing."

"You've never heard of her?"

"She's the woman who was hit by the ambulance."

Applying more pressure, Christopher nodded the anchorman's head. "That's right, Al. Tell me more. Maybe you'd even like to confess."

"She looked familiar to me, but I don't recall ever meeting the woman."

The reporter's hand twitched.

Aarons flinched. "You're pulling out my real hair. If that goes, there won't be anything left to anchor the weave."

"That's right."

"Please. I'm telling the truth. I don't know anything."

"You know something, AA, I'm beginning to believe you."

Christopher released the toupee just before the stage manager came in to say, "One minute to air."

20

"Take two," the stage manager announced.

As Christopher watched the love scene unfold, he wondered what the first take had been like. Why had number two been necessary? One was enough to get any man stirred up. Besides, as far as he was concerned, making love to Susan could never be anything but perfection. There'd be no retakes for him.

Just watching her made him short of breath. When more than his breath began being affected, he deserted the stage in favor of the director's booth. There, he hoped to gain aesthetic distance from Susan's on-camera passion. But the sight of her on six TV screens at once made him feel slightly giddy.

He blinked. He'd never seen such explicit lovemaking on television.

To no one in particular he said, "I didn't know you could get away with that kind of thing."

"Goddammit!" the director shouted. "Quiet in the booth." He swung around his chair, made an obscene gesture, then added, "No tourists allowed, Christopher."

"All right, I'm going." The reporter was on his way out of the booth when he heard the director say, "That does it. I need a break. We'll try another take in ten minutes."

On stage, Susan was breathless. She made a face at Christopher's approach.

"I don't have the time," she said without preamble, then started for her dressing room.

"I've just been watching take two. Since when have they been allowing that on the tube?"

"Only in the afternoons," she said matter-of-factly.

131

"When the kiddies are at school." She eyed him critically. "I suppose now you're jealous."

"Of course not," he lied. "How about dinner tonight?"

"The ambulance is in for repairs, if that's what you're thinking." Her answer was sharp enough to draw blood.

They arrived at her dressing room with Christopher feeling mortally wounded. But maybe she was just tired. Maybe he'd misunderstood.

Once inside, he tried to kiss her. But she turned away impatiently and said, "Bob, I need to be alone to think about the next take."

"What about later tonight?"

She turned to face him. "I'll call you when I feel like company." Her tone was indifferent, her eyes cold.

"The raccoons are fine," Christopher rushed to say, searching for words to cover his pain.

She pushed him out into the hall and closed the door in his face.

Emerging from Stage C a moment later, he looked up into the rain and swore. The harsh words didn't help. The drops continued to feel like tears running down his face.

He shook his head. He'd been a fool. He should have known better. A beautiful woman like Susan, a famous actress, could have her pick of men. So what would she want with an overweight reporter?

The answer to that was obvious. What she'd given him was charity, not love.

By the time he reached his car, he was completely soaked. But worse than the water was the depression that was threatening to drown him. Unfortunately, Christopher knew the antidote for such a mood. Hot fudge sundaes came to mind. Of its own accord, the Mustang headed for the Swensen's ice-cream parlor on Hollywood Boulevard.

But it was slow going. His windshield wipers couldn't cope with the rain at anything over twenty miles an hour. So he crept along, blinked against blurred vision that wasn't entirely due to the weather.

Halfway there, a flooded intersection brought him to a

complete standstill. With traffic backing up behind him, he clenched his teeth and eased the Mustang ahead, crossing his fingers against the possibility of washed out brakes. At two miles an hour even blurred vision and a stomach growling for calories didn't keep him from noticing the church on the corner. Sight of it made him feel like a fool. All along he'd been missing the perfect chance to understand Irma O'Donnell.

Once clear of the intersection, he pressed the speed limit and his eyesight all the way to Highland Park. Knocking on doors, he finally managed to locate the parish church and Irma's priest.

Father Quinn was short and rotund. His hair was unruly and so were his eyes. Beyond giving his name, he said little, though his grimace spoke plainly enough; he distrusted reporters.

To gain the man's confidence, Christopher recounted all that had happened since encountering Irma. When the reporter finished speaking, Father Quinn chuckled and said, "So Irma came to you about St. Christopher, did she?"

They were standing just inside the entrance to a ramshackle wooden church on a block where graffiti were the only paint that had been applied in years.

"She called me her St. Christopher," the reporter said.

"That sounds like Irma all right." The priest's eyes danced wickedly. "She put you on the hook, did she?"

Christopher nodded.

"She was good at that, Irma was. Many's the time she came to me complaining about the church's ruling."

"And what did you do?"

Father Quinn winked. "I helped compose her letters to Rome. I even threw in a little Latin. It didn't help, of course, but it must have startled a few souls in the Vatican."

"Tell me about Irma."

"I can't think about her without thinking of St. Christopher."

"Tell me about St. Christopher then."

"You must understand that anything Irma told me in the confessional is privileged information."

"Even if it would help catch her killer?"

The priest bowed his head, then ran fingers through his wild hair. "If I knew something like that, I'd tell you. But I don't."

"Anything will help right now." As he spoke, Christopher caught his own note of discouragement.

Scratching his head, the priest ushered the reporter to one of the back pews. After genuflecting toward the altar, Quinn joined Christopher on the hard wooden bench, where they sat knee to knee.

During the silence that followed, the priest closed his eyes as if to marshal his thoughts. Then he spoke in hushed tones. "I don't know how many times I sat right here with Irma. And each time it was the same. We'd talk about St. Christopher's fall from grace. I was sympathetic, you understand. I'm not a man to advocate change."

Inside the church, where every word echoed, Christopher felt compelled to whisper. "Do you think she was right?"

"Tradition is a wonderful thing, especially in the Catholic church. We've got two thousand years of it going for us." He paused to run both hands through his hair. "I don't think it's ever a good idea to tamper with tradition. Leave well enough alone, I say. If St. Christopher can fall, what's to stop others from doing the same?"

"I don't remember much about him," the reporter said.

"Ah, it's a wonderful thing, the story of St. Christopher. I guess you'd have to call it a legend now that the church has ruled against him."

Christopher nodded to keep the words coming.

"He fascinated Irma. I can tell you that much." The light in the priest's eyes said he, too, was fascinated by St. Christopher. "According to tradition, Christopher lived in Asia Minor sometime during the third century A.D. He was said to be a man of enormous size and strength who loved God dearly. But he had no talent for preaching, no way to show his love of the Almighty. So he looked around for a way in which to express himself. And finally, after much meditating, an inspiration came to him. He traveled to a river known for its treacherous current, a river where travelers were often swept away while trying to cross."

Father Quinn paused to peer closely at the reporter. "I don't mean to sound like I'm giving a sermon." The priest ducked his head and continued. "After that, Christopher became a human ferry, carrying all those who sought help in crossing the river. For how long this went on, no one knows. Tradition doesn't record that. Suffice it to say that one day a child appeared and asked to be ferried to the other side.

"Ever obliging, Christopher lifted the youngster upon his shoulder and started across. But with every step the burden grew heavier and heavier, until finally Christopher thought they were both doomed, that this was one time the current would win. Yet he refused to give up, struggling with exhaustion until finally they reached the far bank. There he put down the young boy and said, 'Child, thou has put me in dire peril, and hast weighed so heavily on me that if I had borne the weight of the world upon my shoulders it could not have burdened me more.'

"And the child answered, 'Wonder not, Christopher, for not only hast thou borne the whole world on thy shoulders, but Him who created the world.' For it was the Christ child Christopher had carried. And from that time on Christopher became the patron saint of travelers."

The reporter recognized the light in Quinn's eyes. It was the same brightness that had radiated from Irma when Christopher first met her.

The priest slipped to his knees, making Christopher feel uncomfortable for staying on the pew. Quinn bowed his head before going on. "Sometimes Irma said her burden was almost as heavy as St. Christopher's. That burden was her animals and her conscience."

"What burdened her conscience?"

"Telling you about St. Christopher has brought it all back to me. I can't help feeling now that I might have done more for her."

"Like what?"

"I don't know."

"What did she tell you?"

"Irma unburdened herself in the confessional, so there's nothing more I can say."

"I need your help as much as she did."

With a creaking of cartilage, Father Quinn rose to his feet. "When I first saw you at the door, I was suspicious. Irma had spoken so often of you, and in such a way, that you didn't seem real to me. Perhaps I assumed she was exaggerating. Perhaps I was even jealous of the way she revered you. Don't look so startled. Revered is the right word. She didn't say so right out, of course. Not to me. What she did say was that she trusted you, and that you were her good Christopher."

"I don't understand."

"I didn't either at the time. But here you are, trying to help."

"Sure, after it's too late for her."

"It's never too late," Quinn said.

Christopher took that as his cue and got up to leave, but the priest thrust out a restraining hand, touching the gold emblem on the reporter's lapel. "Irma told me that there was good and evil at Channel 3. The evil, she said, was a traveler, but one that the patron saint of travelers would never carry."

21

St. Christopher himself wouldn't have been able to bear the personnel department. Instead of crossing *his* river, they would have redirected its flow until finally the waters petered out in a morass of red tape.

Bob Christopher already felt trapped in such a quagmire as he stepped off the elevator in the network administration building, where personnel took up an entire floor. He paused outside heavy glass doors, trying to think of an alternative. But none came to him, so he stepped inside, immediately confronting a waist-high counter meant to keep out aliens like himself. Beyond that barrier, matching metal desks stretched a good thirty yards, all the way to a glass wall. Beyond the glass, lights blinked from a cobalt-blue computer. Disk drives whirled in matching cabinets.

Christopher readjusted his focus to the nearest desk, where a computer terminal flashed its green-screened language at him, only he was too stupid to understand it. So he called for help.

What he got was an officious-looking woman whose nametag labeled her "D. Francis." Although young, somewhere around thirty, she had the mummified air of an old-fashioned librarian.

"Doris?" he guessed.

"Authorized personnel only," she answered.

Obviously, this was where the real power resided. The programming Channel 3 broadcast over the air each day, including Christopher and his news, was just so much byproduct.

"Dolores?"

"Computers are sensitive to moisture," she said, glaring at his dripping clothes.

He stripped off his raincoat and tossed it back toward the door, where it bunched like a cringing animal.

"Donna?"

Her condemning eyes settled on his lapel emblem. "That gives you no special privileges here."

Quite involuntarily, he backed up a step. The movement brought water squishing from his shoes.

"I'm looking for a name," he explained. "Someone on the lot. I thought your computer might be able to help."

"Impossible. We're in the middle of a payroll run."

"Dorothy?" he queried.

She shook her head.

Christopher grabbed hold of the swinging panel cut in the counter. The woman's immediate response was to clutch at the half door protectively. Then, reluctantly freeing one hand, she pointed in the direction of the computer room. "That's a raised floor out there. Air conditioning ducts are underneath. Get water in there and I don't know what would happen. I really don't."

He kicked off his shoes, then nudged them all the way back to where his coat lay. Instantly, ice began to form between his toes.

Christopher shivered and said, "This is very important. Could I speak to your supervisor?"

"I'm as high as you have to go."

"I'm looking for a murderer." Out loud the statement sounded unlikely as hell. But he persisted nevertheless. "I have several names I want to check out. I think the person I'm after works here on the lot. I don't know where else to go for this kind of information." He hoped he sounded sane.

"If I gave you access to one of our terminals, someone would have to pay for the computer time. You do know how to use a computer terminal, don't you?"

"I'm afraid not."

Her face registered total disbelief. "That means an operator, too. Someone's got to pay."

"I'll write you a check."

"We can't accept money. I need an account number."

"Could I use a phone, please."

She strung an instrument over from the nearest desk, anything to keep him beyond the barrier of her counter. Christopher's fingers were trembling from cold as he dialed Wyn Brewster. But the station manager wasn't in his office, so Reisner was next on the list.

The news director screamed when he heard Christopher's request.

"Herb, I think the answer I need is here."

Reisner sputtered. No doubt his eye was running amok. "How much is all this going to cost?"

D. Francis had no idea. Billing wasn't her area of expertise.

Reisner said no.

Christopher kept after him.

Reisner weakened.

Christopher wheedled.

Reisner said maybe.

Christopher moved in for the kill. "If I'm right, I'll be back on my regular schedule tomorrow."

After a sigh-punctuated pause the news director said, "All right, but only if you promise to be available tomorrow no matter what the computer tells you."

The reporter hesitated to commit himself so totally. Yet he had no option really. If the computer failed to give him an answer, he was out of ideas anyway. "Okay, Herb. It's a deal."

The news director provided a number that satisfied the woman. After that Christopher was allowed beyond the counter. But just barely. As sodden as he was, he was made to stand well back from the desk where D. Francis herself went to work on a terminal keyboard.

He'd been expecting help from a junior clerk. But apparently the woman intended to keep him under personal scrutiny. "Where do you want to begin?" she asked.

"A list of all personnel."

"Network or local?"

"Both, I guess."

"Full or part-time employees?"

"Everybody."

After a squint of condemnation, she began typing. A few seconds later names began appearing on the terminal screen.

"This is the payroll read-out," she said, then touched another key. The names scrolled by quickly.

"Hold it. I can't read that fast."

Two keystrokes started a high-speed printer going. When Christopher approached it, he was warned not to drip into the mechanism. So he sat on the floor rubbing his freezing feet while he waited. Circulation was just starting to come back when she handed him a sheet of computer paper six feet long.

With a sigh, Christopher began going over the single-spaced list.

"How long is this going to take?" she asked.

"I'm looking for someone named Traveler. Or maybe Christopher. Or maybe Saint for that matter. I'm not sure." He did sound insane, and just because of Irma's chance remark to a priest. Perhaps Quinn's memory was faulty. Perhaps . . .

"Why didn't you say so in the first place? I'll punch the names in. The computer will do the searching. That way, we'll save your eyes and my time. Which name should I run first?"

"Christopher of course. You never can tell. Someone on this lot might have the same name I do."

The computer found only one Christopher.

"Try Saint then."

There were no Saints to be found.

That left Traveler, but again the computer came up

empty. Christopher was about to swear when a sneeze overtook him. He sniffled and said, "What's the temperature in here?"

"The computers don't like it over sixty-five."

"Tell that to my news director when I come down with pneumonia."

"May I go back to work now?"

"What about middle names? Or first names? Let's try those."

"The computer isn't programmed to search for names in that fashion."

"Are you saying you can't get me middle and first names?"

"You've already got them on your read-out."

Christopher rubbed his eyes.

"I'll do it again, double-spaced," she volunteered, then went back to her keyboard. Almost immediately the printer began its rapid-fire clatter.

This time the print-out, when she handed it to him, turned out to be over ten feet in length.

"I hate to go out in the rain with this," he told her, fingering the flimsy computer paper. "Is there someplace around here I can read this without freezing to death?"

She smiled for the first time, creating little hollows at the corners of her mouth.

"D as in dimples," he said.

"You can use my office as long as you don't drip on my terminal."

Her office, though small and very businesslike, felt like the tropics by comparison to the bullpen area. Even so, he was still blowing on his hands when she brought him a styrofoam cup brimming with coffee.

"It's not machine coffee," she said. "We make it here, though we really shouldn't. It isn't safe to drink anything around computers. Sometimes I have nightmares about spilling coffee into one of them."

"What is your name?" he asked.

"Danielle."

"When you smile it fits."

Looking embarrassed, she left him alone with the printout.

For a while he ignored the sheet of paper to concentrate on getting coffee inside him. Finally he started reading. After nearly an hour, including a quick double-check, he still hadn't found any of the names. So he went back to Danielle.

"Are you certain I have all personnel?" he asked.

"You have everyone on payroll," she said, "except those paid directly from New York."

"Who are they?"

"Just a few top executives. And of course our network stars. Their pay is supposed to be confidential."

22

CHRISTOPHER DECIDED TO become a spy. There was no other choice. He had to know which one on the confidential list was Irma's wayward traveler. Yet obvious surveillance was out of the question. On a studio lot the size of ABN, word of what he was up to would get around quickly and the killer would be warned.

As it was, Christopher had no proof whatsoever, only the chance remark of an old woman to her parish priest. Then again he wasn't all that certain he wanted proof, not against some of those who came to mind as possibilities. Yet what could he do? He could rationalize Bingo's murder, maybe even Lambert's. He might even be able to come up with an acceptable motive for their killings, but never one that would justify running down an old woman.

At that moment, however, his main worry was catching someone unawares. But a stake-out was out of the question. So all he could do was keep his eye on the next best thing, the center of everything that had been happening, the set of "Emergency Hospital."

Stepping from the administration building, Christopher ran into a wall of rain. He clutched his coat and sprinted for Stage C, wondering if he shouldn't go home and change into dry clothes first. But what was the use in weather like this? Besides, beginning tomorrow he was back on the news no matter what. Once that happened, he might never find the proof he needed. And he wanted proof before risking any kind of personal confrontation.

He was about to duck into a studio when he heard an explosion behind him. Skidding to a halt, he turned around and squinted into the midday gloom. Only when he saw the slicker-clad figure did Christopher realize that he was being shot at. The realization came as the second bullet knocked him down.

After that, he heard the sound of running feet, as if the slicker-man was coming to finish the job. If so, Christopher intended to look death in the face. He turned his head toward the sound, only to land his nose in a deep puddle.

Fear pushed him hard, to the brink of hysteria. Drowned to death by a bullet wasn't an epitaph he could live with. Besides, he knew he couldn't count on anyone from "Emergency Hospital" knowing CPR, or even old-fashioned artificial respiration.

Raising his head to breathe brought enough pain to clear his mind. He had to move, to get out of the line of fire.

Rolling over brought still a new dimension of agony, yet he kept moving while his mouth, of its own accord, opened to draw in breath for a scream. Instead, water rushed in. He sputtered and coughed hard enough to focus the pain. He'd been hit in the left shoulder, not a killing shot at all. Maybe it had never been intended as such. Maybe his suspects were friends after all.

Fool, he swore at himself. *No lies. Not now.* It was insane to think that it had been only a warning shot. Not even Wyatt Earp could be certain of such marksmanship in this weather.

Fueled by anger, Christopher sat up and peered around. There wasn't so much as a slicker in sight. Even the "Wheeler-Dealers" were nowhere to be seen.

With a groan, he brought his right hand up from the puddle to wipe his eyes. As he did so, the fist blossomed with pain, momentarily overriding the shoulder wound.

Blinking rain water from his eyes, he saw the reason. He'd fallen on his right thumb, badly dislocating it. He returned the hand to the numbing water and yelled for help.

None came.

Cursing, he struggled to his feet. Instantly the hand

throbbed back to life. His shoulder let him know it was there too.

He captured his thumb between his teeth, bit down, and yanked. The knuckle snapped into place with a blaze of pain that made him feel as if he were about to burst.

He burst in upon Dr. Janice Owen performing surgery. She almost fainted at the sight of his real blood.

Someone shouted for the first-aid kit. It arrived empty, looted by generations of propmen.

"Call the paramedics," one of the nurses said.

Another surgeon stepped forward. The sight of him, faceless behind his mask, caused Christopher to stumble into Susan.

She dropped her doctor's voice to say, "It's all right, Bob," then led him toward the operating table.

His eyes lost focus. He felt himself sinking down onto a hard surface.

Sound echoed along the dark tunnel of his mind. "Let's get his clothes off."

After a while came the command, "Scalpel."

Susan was going to remove the bullet from his shoulder, but her voice sounded wrong, too masculine.

Then he remembered the masked surgeon and opened his mouth to shout a warning.

"More anesthetic."

After that, he surrendered, thankful that the pain had disappeared. But sadness replaced the pain, sadness born of knowledge. There was no longer any doubt in his mind. The truth could not be denied. Irma's obsession with St. Christopher and the killings were all linked together. Shooting him proved that.

The reporter awoke in a real emergency hospital, with Herb Reisner bending over him saying, "I have a camera crew waiting outside for a bedside statement."

Christopher blinked.

"Compose yourself. It's an exclusive and I want it on our early news."

"What time is it?" The reporter's tongue moved sluggishly.

"We've got about an hour to get the tape back to the studio."

When Christopher didn't reply, the news director began cranking up the bed.

"Who's doing the interview?" the reporter managed to ask.

Reisner kept his head down as if studying the crank mechanism. "On something this big, an exclusive when our own Bob Christopher has deliberately put his life in danger in the line of duty, when—"

"Cut the crap."

"Aarons is waiting outside."

Christopher yelled for a doctor.

"Don't waste time. They need the bed."

"I'm in pain."

"This is an emergency hospital. In and out, that's their policy."

"I'm a gunshot victim."

"That's why Nelson and Duffy are on the way over. I called them myself, after arranging for the crew, of course. From the way they spoke, I figure they have you down for an attempted suicide."

"I've got to get out of here."

"As soon as we do the interview. There's nothing like bedside drama. You know that."

Swearing helped relax Christopher. By the time the camera was set up, he could look at Aarons without screaming.

Reisner rang for the nurse. The moment she came in, she glanced admiringly at the anchorman.

The news director cleared his throat to insure her attention. "Once we begin taping I want you to take the patient's pulse, then just stand there by the bed looking pretty."

As soon as she took up her position, Reisner studied the scene carefully. "Perfect," he said finally. "I couldn't have come up with anything better for Sweeps Week if I'd tried. You're a genius, Bobbo."

Aarons, who'd been quiet and thereby totally out of character, changed as soon as the cameraman said, "Rolling." The verbal cue triggered his adrenaline; his eyes gleamed. His chest swelled as if he were taking on stature rather than air. He snatched up the hand mike and wielded it back and forth between Christopher and himself like a swordsman. To the reporter, it was obvious that AA intended to draw blood. But Christopher paid no attention to the fencing, which was all show, of course, since the lapel microphones were picking up everything anyway.

It was Reisner who insisted that his crews use the big hand-held mikes in the field. He claimed they gave authenticity to interviews while intimidating victims.

But Christopher refused to be intimidated. He lied with a straight face and told them he had no idea who shot him.

After all, what choice did he have? Certainly there was no proof that could withstand any kind of legal test. Nothing to convince the likes of Duffy and Nelson.

But Christopher himself needed no further convincing that he was on the right track. The bullet had seen to that. Now all he wanted was revenge, for himself and for Irma. And to accomplish that he would have to put aside all thoughts of friendship.

The phone rang.

Reisner picked it up gingerly, listened for a moment, then handed the instrument to Christopher. "It's for you."

The AWL voice said, "You were warned. Your war movies have turned this country into an armed camp. And now you are one of the casualties."

"I'm not a soldier."

"You wear Channel 3's uniform. Just following orders is no longer a defense. You've been found guilty by association and condemned to die."

23

CHRISTOPHER SLIPPED HIS Hush Puppies into a pair of footprints at the Chinese Theater. Not only couldn't he fill John Wayne's shoes, the imprints were brimming with enough water to drown the loafers.

A wet-headed shill sidled up and said, "Hey, fella, how would you like to see some real movie stars?"

Shaking his feet, the reporter kept his head down, well beneath his wide-brimmed hat. "Who?" he said, faking enthusiasm.

"Jean Davis for one."

Wrong network.

With mumbled regrets, Christopher moved on to another set of footprints. In weather like this, he knew the networks would be scrambling to raise live audiences. It was just a matter of time before the right recruiter came along.

"Who needs this?" a young woman arrived to say. She was showing a lot of leg, too much for such weather. "There's a way to see Hollywood without getting wet."

Christopher feigned interest.

"A limousine tour of the studios," she explained.

Christopher shook his head before squishing his Hush Puppies across the courtyard, seeking size tens. As he did so, he began to wonder what the hell he was doing there. Sure, he wanted to slip onto the lot unnoticed, but this was going to extremes. Or was it? After all, his last attempt at spying had got him shot.

"It's your lucky day," a young man said, pulling Christopher right out of Ronald Reagan's footsteps. "I can get you into one of ABN's new sitcoms. Normally, there's standing room only. But as I say, this is your lucky day."

Translated, that meant the producers were desperate for live audiences, despite the fact that such souls tended to cough and squirm through retakes and sometimes even ignored prompter signs.

"I don't think so," Christopher responded, playing hard to get.

The shill's head swiveled nervously as he took a quick glance around. The pickings were meager. What few tourists there were looked like refugees from something worse than television.

"Do you like cops and robbers?" the recruiter asked, a touch of desperation in his voice.

Christopher shrugged a maybe.

"Hey, come on. Give me a chance. I'm talking big stars here and a brand new show that's never been seen before."

The reporter smiled.

"You ever heard of Evan Paul?"

Christopher nodded yes, though he had no idea who Paul might be.

"Well, he's left the movies to do TV for ABN. The show's called 'Fuzzy, Was He?' Get it? Cops, fuzz." The shill looked smug, like a man who'd just played an unbeatable trump.

"I don't know," Christopher said but allowed himself to be led toward a bus at the curb.

Sensing victory, the recruiter let go with his clincher. "A free lunch goes with it."

Christopher stepped aboard the bus, where he had to wait nearly an hour before there were enough passengers to make the drive to the studio worthwhile.

Once on the lot, the passengers were herded into an audience holding area, still littered with fall-out from "Wheeler-Dealers." Overhead, rain drummed on the corrugated roof. The noise seemed to agitate the crowd. Christopher caught some of their anxiety and for a moment wondered if he was acting foolish by sneaking on his own lot. But then someone jostled his wounded shoulder, reminding him what happened to exposed targets.

149

"What time is the show?" the jostling man asked in a rush of wine breath.

A uniformed page, complete with logoed umbrella, hurried forward to say, "Just a few minutes now, sir." Probably never before had wine breath been called sir.

As soon as Christopher saw additional pages arrive with complimentary coffee and hot chocolate, he knew they were in for a long wait. No doubt "Wheeler-Dealers," which used the same studio, had run over. The reporter could think of no other reason for the audience to be kept waiting. If the delay had been merely technical, the drinks would have been served inside.

But the holdup suited Christopher perfectly. From where he was standing, he had an unobstructed view of the main entrance to Stage C, his primary target for the moment. As the home of "Emergency Hospital," it was the key to everything. The attempt on his life had proved that.

Christopher was still trying to visualize his suspects carrying guns when the taping call came for "Fuzzy, Was He?" As the audience surged forward, eager to be on the move at last, he slipped away unnoticed, taking shelter in a 1941 olive-drab Ford sedan, part of the equipment that had been moved onto the studio streets in anticipation of tomorrow's remake of World War II.

Almost as soon as he slipped inside the car, the windows steamed up, making him wonder if he wasn't radiating heat from a fever. But when he cracked open a side window, he realized the weather had changed dramatically in the last few minutes. The temperature was up. Maybe the storm was about to break at last.

He closed his eyes, dreaming of sunshine. After a few moments, he felt himself sweating. Maybe the wound had become infected. Maybe . . .

His eyes snapped open. Nervously he wiped condensation from the window. Then he pressed his face against the cool glass to watch the bright blue-and-white "Emergency Hospital" ambulance ease away from Stage C's loading dock. Passing the parked convoy of olive drab, the ambulance looked totally out of place. Its driver, too, appeared improbable, dressed as she was in a low-cut, yellow tanktop.

Susan Arthur stared straight ahead as she maneuvered the ambulance around an assortment of armored cars and Jeeps. Apparently she didn't even see Christopher when he waved at her. A shout died in his throat. Where was she going in *their* ambulance?

He knew he had to find out. The '41 Ford's key was in the ignition. The engine, probably newer than the car, started immediately. He accelerated like a teenager, banging through speed-bumps at the main gate hard enough to rip something loose underneath the car. Metal clanged as he fishtailed onto Wheeler Drive, heading west toward the center of Hollywood.

At the first intersection, the ambulance turned north on a quiet residential street. The instant he lost sight of the vehicle, Christopher panicked, stomping on the accelerator. The Ford spun out of control. By the time he righted the car and reached the corner, he turned too quickly and ran one tire up over the curb. A hubcap clattered away. The engine died.

If it hadn't been for the rain, half the neighborhood would have come out to see the show. As it was, he doubted that anyone had even heard the noise. Certainly Susan wouldn't have, a block ahead as she was.

He restarted the engine just as the ambulance pulled into a driveway in the middle of the next block. Easing the Ford into gear, he crept along until he was across the street from Susan.

She remained in the driver's seat without moving. Steam coming from the exhaust told him the engine was still idling. After a moment, she leaned over and opened the passenger door onto a short flight of steps leading to a Hoover bungalow.

Christopher scrunched down in his seat and prayed that Susan wouldn't look back and catch him spying on her. But apparently she had eyes only for the man who trotted

151

down the steps and climbed in beside her. Almost immediately the ambulance rolled down the driveway and into an open garage.

Christopher saw the exhaust die. He switched off the Ford's engine and waited. Only a few seconds passed before the man reappeared to pull down the garage door, closing himself, the ambulance, and Susan inside.

The reporter grabbed hold of the steering wheel until his arms shook with the effort. The vibrations set off fresh twinges of agony in his shoulder. Only now, he welcomed the physical pain; it helped deaden his thoughts. But only for a moment.

Drive away, he told himself. Forget her.

He glared at his clenched fingers, willing them to relax. But even when they came away from the steering wheel, they balled into fists aching to lash out at someone.

"You know what has to be done."

Inside the closed car, the sound of Christopher's voice was high-pitched and hollow and took him totally by surprise. He hadn't been aware of moving his lips. And now that the words were out he wanted to deny them, wanted to protest that he didn't know what had to be done. But he did.

Swallowing against a growing taste of bile, he opened the door of the old Ford. He had the feeling that his body was acting on its own, that his brain had ceased to function. Any man with brains would drive away.

He stepped out of the car. The rain, he realized for the first time, had stopped. But low clouds remained, bringing on an early dusk. Lights were already on in houses throughout the neighborhood.

Common sense told him the driveway couldn't be more than seventy-five feet long. But in the fading light his eyes, abetted by conscience, said otherwise. It would take him forever to make such a trek, and all the while he would be fully exposed to the neighbors' lighted windows that were already casting bright rectangles onto the concrete driveway.

An impossible task, he decided, as he began creeping toward the garage. With the rain gone, he had only the dripping drain pipes to mask the sounds he made. To his own ears, each footfall seemed thunderous.

Just outside the first rectangle of light, he hesitated. What the hell was he going to do when he reached the garage anyway? Throw open the door and yell, "Surprise?"

With a shrug that sent a thrill of pain through him, Christopher lurched forward, squinting against the brightness. Anyone looking out the window would be certain to see him. But his luck held. No shouts came. So he took a deep breath and plunged through the last two brilliant patches.

When his fingers closed on the garage door's handle, he froze. His brain sent the proper signal for the muscles to act, but somewhere along the way the order got short-circuited. The door stayed closed.

With a sigh, he moved around to the side of the garage, which was now deep in shadow, and groped along a stucco wall until he found a window. Pressing his face against the glass, he strained to catch the slightest glimpse of what was going on inside. But he saw nothing but blackness.

In desperation, he pressed his ear against the pane. Still nothing.

His fingers came up to explore the window frame, then went on to test each square of glass. There was no way in.

He moved farther along the wall, his hands feeling the way. At the rear of the garage he found another window. This time his fingers discovered an opening where a small pane of glass had been broken out.

Once he'd checked for sharp edges, Christopher moved his ear against the opening. At first he heard nothing. Then gradually the sounds coming from inside grew, until finally he wanted to cover his ears. Susan had uttered those same sounds when making love to him in the back of the ambulance.

24

THE NEXT DAY the sun was bright enough to kill vampires, though Christopher would have preferred a wooden stake for Reisner's heart. The news director was jubilant. He threw his arms around Christopher and squeezed.

Pain sagged the reporter's knees. But Reisner didn't notice. He was aiming a kiss when Christopher staggered out of the way.

"Look at that sign," Reisner said, pointing to his THINK MEAN plaque.

For a moment, Christopher couldn't focus, so intense was his hangover. He'd spent half the night futilely trying to drink Susan out of his system.

"Inspiration," Reisner murmured. "That's what it is."

After blinking repeatedly, Christopher was able to oblige the news director and concentrate on the plaque. And so did Channel 3's sales manager, Ed Flemming, who was lounging on Reisner's sofa.

"The day I put up that sign I stopped being a nice guy," Reisner expounded. "And from that moment on our ratings started going up."

Wiping pain-induced sweat from his brow, Christopher said, "Are you trying to tell me that Sweeps are in?"

"Do you hear him?" Reisner asked Flemming. "Are the Sweeps in?" The news director's eye rolled as he rushed at Christopher for another hug. The reporter escaped by sitting down.

"Tell him," Flemming said, his tone smug, his gloating grin enough to turn the reporter's already queasy stomach.

"No more Mr. Nice Guy," Reisner shouted.

The sales manager waved a press release. "Four full points in news alone. Do you realize what that means?"

"That Al Aarons will become insufferable."

The news director laughed. "When he gets out of hand, we'll trot out one of those old video tapes of his."

"Four points," Flemming rhapsodized. "That works out to more than four million dollars in additional revenue during the coming year." He rubbed his fingers as if already counting the money.

"Just how much of that goes into your pocket?" Christopher asked.

Reisner answered. "There's a lot more than money at stake here. Ed has just been promoted."

The reporter groaned. "To what?"

The sales manager stood up and did a half turn as if seeking admiration. "Do I look any different?"

"Now that you mention it," Reisner jumped in, "there is a certain aura about you."

Christopher couldn't tell if the news director was being funny or obsequious.

Reisner made a trumpeting sound. "You're looking at our new boss."

Christopher swallowed an obscenity while the news director made a production out of shaking hands with Flemming. No doubt they'd been practicing before Christopher arrived.

"Ed's just been named station manager," Reisner said.

"What about Wyn Brewster?"

"Moved up to network vice president. It's all in the press release."

Flemming flaunted a sheaf of paper.

"New York?" Christopher asked.

"With bells on," the news director said. "As of now, Brewster's made the bigtime. He's in charge of network programming."

Abruptly Christopher stepped forward and snatched the press release from Flemming's hand. Ignoring Reisner's snort of protest, the reporter turned his back on the two men and began reading the lengthy announcement. In addition to the usual puffery, there was extensive detail.

It wasn't only the local news that had scored a ratings victory. Programming throughout Channel 3's daily schedule had surged ahead. Even "Emergency Hospital" had moved up two positions to become number one in its time slot.

"When were the ratings announced?" Christopher asked.

"First thing this morning," Reisner answered.

"It's only ten now." The reporter waved the press release. "This is fast work, isn't it?"

Flemming glared. "If it's any of your business, we were tipped in advance."

"I thought ratings were a closely guarded secret."

The new station manager exchanged glances with Reisner, who then looked pleadingly at Christopher. The reporter shrugged. Flemming was already an enemy. "You haven't answered my question."

"As I recall," Reisner said quickly, "you're back on regular daily assignment. Maybe you'd better start working."

"That's all right," Flemming said. "I'll answer his questions. I wouldn't want him to think we had anything to hide." His lips drew back, exposing the best orthodontists had to offer. "We did get some inside information a few hours ahead of time. That's no crime. There's certainly no way we can profit from it. You can't sell a Sweeps book until it's official."

"And just how did you get this inside information?"

"You don't really expect an answer to that, do you?"

"Tell me this then. Did you make all the arrangements yourself?"

Flemming hesitated a moment too long before saying yes. Perhaps it took him that long to adjust to the fact that as station manager he was now responsible for everything that went on at Channel 3.

In that same span of time, another kind of enlightenment came to Christopher. The reason for murder suddenly became clear to him. He went back to the press release, which also included a detailed account of all impending promotions, complete with executive biographies. Names were fully spelled out, a sight which made the reporter sick to his stomach. He knew the killer now, a killer with the middle name of Traveler. Irma's Traveler who was too great a burden for even St. Christopher to bear.

Without a word, the reporter turned and left the office. In the streets outside, propmen, stagehands, technicians of all kinds were glorying in the first real sunshine in weeks. Even the soldiers getting ready for World War II looked cheerful.

But Christopher felt no joy whatsoever as he headed for the National Rating Service, which had offices on Sunset Boulevard.

The building, three stories of grimy stucco and smog-dulled aluminum, was at least twenty years old, ancient by Southern California standards.

NRS occupied only one floor, the second. Getting off the elevator, Christopher felt cheated somehow. A rating service wielding so much power ought to have an entire building to itself.

But the receptionist, a middle-aged woman without makeup or attempted glamor, changed his mind. NRS was too sure of itself, too secure in its authority, to have need of glamorous facades.

"You're Bob Christopher, aren't you?" the woman said. "I watch you on the news."

Recognition put an end to anything but frontal assault.

"There's someone I want to see."

She smiled, only too happy to help.

"I don't know his name. I'll have to look around."

Her desk barred the way to a short hallway, off which opened half a dozen glass doors. Christopher started toward the nearest one.

"Please," she said quietly. "I have to announce you."

"I'm sorry," he replied and opened the door.

It took him four doors to find the familiar face, the one belonging to the man from the Hoover bungalow, Susan's lover.

By now, Christopher had collected a crowd. Even so, he had to admire their restraint. Nobody laid a hand on him. Even loverboy looked apologetic when he asked Christopher to leave.

The reporter would have preferred violence.

"What's your name?" the reporter demanded.

"Why do you want to know?"

"I'm an admirer of your work."

"I know who you are, but we've never met."

"Don't be too sure of that." Christopher was about to reveal the circumstances when he felt a gentle tap on his shoulder.

Ignoring the pain from his wound, the reporter whirled around, ready to take a punch. But he deflated at the sight of an elderly man, whose white feathery mustache looked as if it were about to blow away.

"What seems to be the trouble?" he asked, fluttering the feather precariously.

"It must be the ratings," someone declared.

The elderly man shook his head. "Channel 3 did better than anyone expected."

Suddenly Christopher felt the fight go out of him, but not the anger. Real revenge, he decided, was better than breaking noses. He scowled at Susan's lover and said, "I've made a mistake. I thought I knew you."

The white-haired man sighed with obvious relief. This was something he could deal with. "That's our Mr. Franks. He's in charge of programming our computers."

Christopher arrived back at Channel 3 in time to see the battle lines forming. Tanks, complete with swastikas, had been rented for the occasion. Opposing them were muddy GI's, armed with only a few bazookas. Their victory would be due to stealth and darkness.

Originally, the battle was to have been shot day-for-night, but the bright sunshine made matching earlier scenes impossible. So the director had called a halt until darkness. In the meantime, moving around the lot was like being in the middle of a war.

Christopher entered the newsroom carrying a flag of surrender.

"I'm not taking prisoners," Reisner called out. "Not after what you did to me." He hustled the reporter away from the assignment area.

"I'm sorry about Flemming," Christopher said softly so they wouldn't be overheard. "But the man hates me anyway."

The news director closed one eye. "What's done is done. In the meantime, you had a deal with me, remember? Beginning today, you were supposed to be back on the news live. In fact, your first report is scheduled for the 'Six O'Clock.' "

"I've got most of the answers now. It's just a matter of tying everything together."

"I suppose that means you won't be ready in time."

"I'm not enjoying this, Herb. I wish I could walk away. But it's too late now."

"You're in trouble, Christopher. You haven't got Wyn Brewster to run to anymore. From now on, Flemming is going to be looking for an excuse to dump you."

From the assignment desk, Wayne Gossett shouted for help.

Reisner responded with an obscene gesture. "He probably wants me to hold his hand, or maybe tell him what a great job he's doing."

"We all need that sometimes," Christopher said, but he knew there would be no praise for what he had to do, not even from himself.

"Fire!" Gossett called.

"When he yells rape, I'll see what he wants."

"Where's F-Stop?"

"I take it you need an accomplice?"

"If I'm right, it will be over tonight."

Reisner looked as if he were about to object. Then he leaned forward to peer into Christopher's face. "The last time I saw your cameraman he was on overtime drinking coffee . . . in my office."

F-Stop Fitzgerald had taken the THINK MEAN sign down and was about to deface it with gum when Christopher walked in.

"I need you tonight," the reporter announced.

"Great."

"Not so fast. What I have in mind could be dangerous."

"We've been there before."

"Nothing like this."

F-Stop shrugged.

"Besides, this will be on our own time."

The cameraman dotted the "i" with spearmint before replying. "I hope you don't need a soundman, because Scanlon won't go for anything without overtime."

Christopher explained exactly what he had in mind, concluding, "You can still back out."

F-Stop grinned. "You couldn't keep me away. Besides, I've always wanted to violate union rules by handling the sound myself."

With that he left to gather the necessary equipment.

Once Christopher was alone, he began experimenting with his voice. After a few moments, he decided that a hoarse whisper would be the best disguise.

He picked up the internal phone and dialed the Executive Bungalow. Unexpectedly Susan answered. When he didn't respond immediately to her hello she demanded, "Who is this?"

Christopher took a deep breath. His whisper squeaked a little. "Just call me the Sweeps Fairy."

"What?" Fear tainted the query.

"I want a thousand dollars. Otherwise, I tell everyone that the fix was in."

"I don't know what you're talking about."

"About you and Franks and his computers at NRS."

"I . . ." Susan's voice was high-pitched and on the verge of cracking.

"The first payment is due today," he whispered.

"Who is this?"

"Think of me as Irma O'Donnell's stand-in," Christopher said, hoping he'd guessed correctly. After all, Irma had spoken of a bonus, of dirty money. And blackmail was as dirty as you could get.

"If you don't tell me who this is, I'm hanging up."

Please do, Christopher prayed. Hang up and prove you don't know what I'm talking about. He let thirty seconds go by before asking, "Are you still there?"

Her ragged breathing said yes.

"Payment is to be delivered at seven tonight on the back lot."

In the middle of World War II, he added to himself.

"Where?"

"Just be there," he said, his whisper on the verge of slipping into something more recognizable. "I'll find you." His hand was clenching the phone so hard that his entire body shook with the effort.

"I don't know what you're talking about," Susan said lamely and hung up.

But not, Christopher reminded himself, before she had all the necessary information. All she had to do now was pass it on, because certainly she wouldn't be the one to show up at seven o'clock.

For a moment the reporter had trouble prying his fingers loose from the phone. Finally he left the office to find F-Stop. He wanted them both in position early.

161

25

ROMMEL DIDN'T LOOK right. Certainly nothing like James Mason. And anyone else, as far as Christopher was concerned, was an impostor. Of course, ABN couldn't have afforded James Mason, even if he was still available. But the network had managed hundreds of extras in uniform, not to mention trucks, armored cars, tanks, and even Nazi motorcycles with sidecars. In addition, the battlefield was strewn with burnt-out hulks, plywood replicas courtesy of the Props Department.

All in all, the scene looked quite warlike. And Christopher fit right in, dressed as a wounded GI. Only the bandages on his arm were real.

To get away with such a deception, he had bribed an assistant director. The price was a date with Karen Kamura, the beautiful co-anchor of "The Five O'Clock News," even though Christopher had no idea whether he could deliver her or not. He'd also tossed in his season tickets to the Raiders games.

The tickets bought him something extra, protective camouflage in the form of half a dozen soldiers that AD kept lounging near a disabled Tiger Tank, a rental that had developed engine trouble and was therefore out of the war.

Christopher had selected the broken-down panzer as his observation post. From there, he had clear fields of fire in all directions.

What he hadn't planned on was the movie's director, a maniac who called for fire hoses just as it was getting dark. He wanted rain to match scenes filmed earlier in the week.

Spray from the hoses, when it came, covered a large area of the battlefield, but all of it was a long way from

Christopher's observation post. The AD shouted an apology just before a megaphone-amplified voice ordered the reporter's battle-weary companions into the wet fray.

As they trudged away into B-movie oblivion, Christopher spoke into his wireless microphone. "F-Stop, can you hear me?"

"I've got you in my sights." The cameraman sounded so loud that Christopher adjusted his earwig, a Telex intercom system linking him with F-Stop, who had set up his gear atop a filming platform on the other side of the battlefield.

"Is the light good enough?"

"No problem."

"And you'll be able to distinguish faces?"

"With this lens, Bobbo, you look like you're standing right next to me."

"Just keep me in sight, that's all."

"Okay, but don't get behind the tank."

"Someone's coming," Christopher whispered, removing the earwig and checking to make certain his wireless mike didn't show.

The SS uniform, complete with Iron Cross, looked real and so did the Luger, which was pointed straight at the reporter. Christopher's worst fear had become reality. Confronting him was his friend, Wyn Brewster. Wyn T. Brewster. Middle initial "T" as in Traveler, Irma's evil wayfarer who was so unacceptable to St. Christopher.

The reporter took a step toward the Luger. He had to get within microphone range.

"Hold it. This gun is loaded with real bullets, not movie blanks."

"I believe you." Christopher froze in place, praying that F-Stop could boost the sound electronically if necessary.

"I'm sorry, Bob. As soon as Susan told me about the call, I knew it had to be you. I guess I've been waiting for it all along."

"Why couldn't it have been Flemming?"

"He doesn't have the brains. Anything beyond padding

163

an expense account is too much for him. Now a real fiddle, that takes some doing."

"How long have you been fiddling with the ratings?"

"You're too good a reporter for someplace like Channel 3."

"Are you making me a better offer?"

"Believe me, I'd love to take you to New York with me. But I know you too well. That conscience of yours isn't to be trusted."

An amplified voice swept over them. "All right everybody, to your places. We've only got a couple of hours before the neighbors start complaining."

Christopher turned to watch the war. Out of the corner of his eye, he caught Brewster doing the same thing.

"Are we ready?" the director boomed over his bullhorn.

No one said otherwise.

"Action."

Explosions preceded a German counterattack.

Now was the time, Christopher thought. No one could possibly hear a single shot.

The detonations stopped.

"Cut, cut," yelled the director. "The tanks were late on their cue. Reset the scene."

"A reprieve," Brewster announced. "Next time, I'm afraid, I'll have to make use of the diversion." He waved the Luger to emphasize his point.

Christopher had to hurry if he wanted F-Stop to get everything. "The ratings might have gone up on their own, Wyn."

"Don't kid yourself. You think journalism will win out in the end. No way, my friend. It's all showbiz. Showbiz and money and buying the right people. That was the only way I was going to get out of here. Hell, the powers that be have never given me enough money to compete with the other network stations in this town." The Luger trembled slightly. "New York doesn't seem to understand. You can't make those million-dollar ratings points without spending something up front. Not honestly anyway. So now, all of a sudden, the big brass at ABN think I'm some kind of low-budget miracle worker."

"What happens when you get to New York and can't produce any more cheap miracles?"

"I'll think of something."

"Like Susan?"

"The mark of a good executive is to use his people to their best advantage. And Susan just happens to be very talented on her back."

Christopher spoke through clenched teeth. "You used her."

Brewster laughed, a short, sharp burst. "Me? She wants a hell of a lot more out of life than her role on 'Emergency Hospital.' Hellsakes, she jumped at the chance to help. Naturally, as the new head of network programming, I'll be able to personally supervise her career from now on."

"Who else will she have to sleep with?"

The Luger flicked back and forth. "I've known how you felt about her for a long time, Bob. Because of that, she wasn't part of my original plan, not until that NRS bastard Franks wanted more than money. He wanted Susan."

Christopher had trouble making his tongue work for a moment. Finally he managed to get out, "Your mistake was the ambulance. I followed Susan when she drove it to meet Franks."

"He was terrified of being discovered. Of course Susan didn't want him at her place, and Franks lives with his mother." Brewster smiled crookedly. "They did use Susan's dressing room once. But that's when all the trouble started. Old Irma caught them at it. She was a cagy bird. She followed Franks when he left and found out just how important he was. That was when she decided she needed help in her blackmail scheme. So she let Lambert in on it."

"Why would she do that?"

"Oh, yes. I keep forgetting. You think she was something special. Well, she was, in her own crazy way. She

165

had a crush on Lambert. And Mark, being what he was, played up to her. He used to keep the stage crew entertained with his antics. Once, he even kissed that St. Christopher medal of hers."

Brewster paused momentarily to catch his breath. "How they found out that Franks was with NRS I don't know. But they did. So from then on we had to be more careful. Susan suggested motels. But Franks wouldn't go anywhere public. And that was fine by me. After all, we couldn't take a chance that the rating service would get wise. So I came up with the ambulance. Franks found it a real turn-on. Susan, too, for that matter."

Christopher could testify to that. "But I followed the ambulance right to Franks's front door."

"That place where they met?" Brewster shook his head. "No way, my friend. That house is owned by ABN. Slowly but surely the network is buying up the whole area. We've got to. You heard the director. The neighbors are complaining about noise on the back lot. Pretty soon there won't be any neighbors."

"But why the ambulance?"

"We could move it around, never the same place twice. People wouldn't get suspicious that way, or so we thought." Brewster's eyes sparkled. He was like a man on drugs, but his was the ultimate high, power. And he had to brag about his accomplishments. "To tell you the truth, Bob, we—"

A shriek of feedback cut him off. "Let's go!" The director's voice boomed across the lot. "Get those charges set. This isn't the Battle of the Bulge."

When the echo died away, Christopher asked, "Why did you have to kill them?"

Brewster laughed. And a nasty sound it was, too. "For a reporter, you're so damned naïve sometimes."

Christopher forced himself to smile back. "You haven't answered my question."

"Poor Bobbo," Brewster mocked. "And all the time Irma pretended the blackmail money wasn't for herself, but for her animals. She thought she was a regular St. Francis of Assisi. But with feet of clay, eh. Saints don't blackmail people, now do they. Isn't that right, St. Christopher?" Brewster slapped his thigh. "Hell, old Irma was not only a blackmailer, she was a whore. As for Lambert, I would never have been able to satisfy his ambition."

The reporter shook his head in disbelief.

"There are times when you aren't to be believed, Bobbo," Brewster told him. "Life isn't a fairy tale and you're not some kind of knight. The answer to Irma has been right there under your nose all the time. You just didn't look at Aarons's tape closely enough."

The Luger came up.

"I'd hate to die ignorant. At least explain about Bingo."

"Ever the reporter, eh Bobbo? Well, what the hell? I'll let you die happy. Bingo was no better than the old lady. For all I know he was her partner in the blackmail scheme. They had Al Aarons nailed to the wall, and I couldn't let that happen. If it did, it would have looked phony as hell to be rated number one in the middle of an anchor change."

Christopher wanted to ask for more detail, for more clarification. But he didn't dare interrupt the flow of words.

"As for that clumsy disguise of Bingo's. Hell, a good station manager knows what's happening on his lot. I got a call from props as soon as Bingo stepped out the door wearing the nun's outfit."

Brewster clicked his tongue at the reporter. "So I didn't have to stand around in the rain like you did, Bobbo. No, sir. I was waiting for Bingo in props, nice and dry all the time. You should have seen his face when he saw me. Got down on his knees, he did, and handed over the twenty-five thousand, which is going to come in handy in New York I can tell you."

As soon as Brewster paused, the reporter asked, "And Lambert?"

"Killing that bastard should have been an end to it. As a blackmailer, he was a typical actor. You know how he wanted his payoff? In the form of a raise. How the hell

167

was I going to deliver that? Network policy is quite clear. You write actors out before they become too high-priced. So when Lambert came to me with his demands, I didn't really have any choice." Brewster chuckled. "When I wore that surgeon's outfit, I set him up perfectly, even if I do say so myself. And just think. I kept him in character, since he'd already committed murder on the soap. Hellsakes, Bobbo, you're the only reason my plan didn't work. You wouldn't buy Lambert's suicide. Too bad saints like yourself long to become martyrs."

"Speaking for myself, I'd be perfectly happy to accept a bribe."

Brewster's face twisted into a half smile. "Why is it I don't believe you?"

"Irma wasn't the only one with animals to feed. You can ask Susan. She wouldn't want anything to happen to me or my raccoons."

Toying with his Iron Cross, Brewster appeared to consider the reporter's plea. "And just how much would it take to keep you quiet?"

If he was going to stay alive for the next few minutes, Christopher had to come up with something believable.

"You two," someone called. An assistant director was approaching, and not the one Christopher had bribed. "We're paying you good money, so join the battle."

"My friend here is sick," Brewster said. "I was just helping him to the first aid station."

Christopher shook his head, trying to will the man to see the truth of the situation.

The AD's cheeks puffed before he shook a fist at them. "Get out of the way then. You're in our shot when we pan the battlefield."

In the distance, the director coughed into his bullhorn. "Are we ready?"

"Damn," the AD said. "Get behind the tank and stay there until we finish this scene." He trotted back toward the main shooting platform.

Gesturing with the Luger, Brewster marched Christopher toward the panzer. Once the metal monster was between them and the director, not to mention F-Stop, Brewster ordered Christopher down on his haunches in the mud.

Off balance because of his wounded shoulder, the reporter slipped as he tried to ease into the goo. When he reached out to steady himself, the wireless mike jiggled out from beneath his olive drab lapel.

Brewster's jaw dropped open. An obscenity exploded from his slack mouth; his eyes took on a crazy glint, causing Christopher to catch his breath.

The obscenity was blown away by the director's thunderous, "Stand by!"

With Luger outstretched, Brewster moved forward until the pistol was within inches of the reporter's forehead. Then the muzzle dropped slightly toward the miniature microphone. "Who . . ." was all he got out before the director's "Action" restarted World War II.

Explosions shook the ground. Tank engines revved and roared. Rifle and machine gun fire provided accompaniment.

Christopher tasted bile.

A few moments later the shouts of charging infantry signaled victory. A quiet descended on the battlefield.

"That's a take," the director announced, sounding like the voice of God.

Brewster's hands were trembling, but not so badly that the Luger, up close as it was, ever left Christopher's head. After a sharp intake of breath, the new vice president of ABN programming spoke into the microphone. "Whoever's out there taping this had better come forward. Otherwise, I shoot Christopher here and now."

"Stay where you are," Christopher told F-Stop.

Brewster chopped the pistol barrel against the reporter's jaw. Pain exploded inside Christopher's head. Blood ran down his chin and began dripping onto his uniform.

"I didn't expect the mike," Brewster said. "I admit that. But with you, I should have known."

He pressed the Luger muzzle against Christopher's nose, then used his free hand to unclip the wireless microphone. After that, Brewster stepped back a pace and closed his hand around the tiny piece of equipment. "I also took precautions."

He raised his fist and gestured toward the scenic warehouse. Almost against his will, Christopher twisted around to see what would happen.

A soldier emerged from the building and headed their way. The GI's walk was all wrong, and he carried his M 1 Rifle at an odd angle.

When the director announced, "Everyone into position for close-ups," the GI broke into a jog. At that moment Christopher realized it was Susan in uniform.

She arrived out of breath.

Brewster knocked the rifle from her grasp and pushed her into the mud beside the reporter. Then the vice president smiled and said, "All right, Bob. I'll shoot her if your friend doesn't join us."

Christopher stared at Susan. She looked startled, scared even. Perhaps she really was in danger. But she was also an actress, so he couldn't trust the emotion showing in her face.

Brewster opened his fist, exposing the microphone. "Well?" he demanded.

Christopher said nothing.

Brewster's smile made the reporter squirm. "Say something, Susan, or your pretty face is going to look just like Bob's."

Susan sobbed.

Brewster held out the mike.

Susan pleaded.

Brewster clarified. "I'll shoot them both if you don't come running, F-Stop. It is you, isn't it, Fitzgerald? I mean who else would Bobbo trust? Oh, and F-Stop, bring the video tape with you, please."

The *please* was shattering. For such a polite word, it

held more menace than anything Brewster had said so far.

"It's a trick," Christopher said for F-Stop's benefit. "Stay there. You're our insurance."

Brewster tossed the small microphone toward Susan. As she reached for it, his open hand struck her face.

She screamed. The mike plopped into the mud but didn't sink.

"It's no trick," Brewster assured. "And I won't wait very long either."

He retrieved the microphone and pocketed it.

"May I get up now?" Susan said.

"Better not," Brewster answered. "Not until F-Stop gets here."

Her expression said squatting in the mud had not been part of her plan. But she kept at it, playing her role, until Fitzgerald arrived. Only then did she look Christopher in the face. What he saw in her eyes made him shrivel inside.

Rubbing her cheek, Susan struggled to her feet. "You didn't need to hit me so hard, Wyn."

"I wanted a real scream." Brewster took the tape cassette from the cameraman. "Is this the only copy?"

"What do you think we are?" F-Stop answered. "CBS?"

"Down on your knees," Brewster ordered. "Next to your pal there."

Susan stared disgustedly at her mud-covered fatigues. "I need a bath."

"Later. Right now we're going to wait for the fighting to continue. When it does"—he brandished the Luger—"we'll provide a couple of extra casualties. Think of it, Bob, you'll make the news yet. You might even provide enough publicity to jump 'Battleguard's' ratings a couple of points."

"What about me?" F-Stop asked.

"I'm afraid cameramen don't have the drawing power of on-camera personnel."

"I don't like waiting here," Susan complained.

"I'm sure our friends in the mud are in no hurry."

171

Brewster tilted his head as if to catch the echo of his words. "I'm really sorry about this, Bob. I hope you believe that. But what choice do I have."

"I'm sorry, too," Christopher said. But his words were for F-Stop. "I shouldn't have gotten you into this."

The cameraman shrugged. "I figured it was a trap. That's why I sent our soundman for help."

Christopher closed his eyes to keep from giving away the bluff. Even if their soundman, Floyd Scanlon, had been on the scene, he would have been totally useless. He never listened to what was being recorded, but contented himself with occasional glances at the VU meter to make certain the decibel levels were registering.

"I don't believe it," Brewster said, but doubt showed in his face. He was, after all, a creature of television. And ABN's union contract called for two technicians on all camera crews, one handling video, the other audio.

Keeping the Luger at the ready, he climbed onto the tank and peered toward the shooting platform. "I don't see anything."

"Scanlon is long gone," F-Stop said matter-of-factly.

"Where?"

"To call the police."

Even while sliding back down from the turret, Brewster managed to keep the Luger aiming at them. Once again, he seemed perfectly self-assured. "I'm not buying it."

Susan said, "Bob, I didn't have anything to do with what's happening. That's the truth."

"And Franks?"

"Okay, so I slept with him. But that was only business. I didn't know about the killings." She shook her head sadly just as Dr. Janice Owen so often did when learning of the untimely death of one of her patients. "I didn't even know Wyn was being blackmailed."

The reporter looked skeptical.

"Okay, so he finally told me. But that was because he wanted to make me an accomplice."

Brewster chuckled, a sound devoid of humor. "Do you believe her, Bobbo?" He winked.

The character of Dr. Janice Owen began to crumble.

"My dear Susan," Brewster said reassuringly. "You can stop worrying. I'll take care of the soundman if it comes to that. Just remember, he doesn't have any proof. We have the videotape right here."

"That's a blank," the cameraman said. "Scanlon has the real one."

"Good, Fitzgerald. Very good. But you see, I've remembered something important. Bob once told me about that soundman of yours. Neither of you trust him, so I doubt very much that he was ever out there." He waved the Luger toward the battlefield. "And if he was, he won't make a very convincing witness even if he does fall into the wrong hands."

"We can't take the chance," Susan said.

"We have no other choice," Brewster responded. "So let's get this over with." His arm stretched out, bringing the Luger ever closer to Christopher.

And that was when F-Stop made his move, lunging from his kneeling position in the mud. Only Brewster was too fast. There was a muffled explosion as the pistol went off against the cameraman's chest.

Out of reflex or determination, Christopher didn't know which, F-Stop grabbed hold of Brewster's arm. The Luger flopped in the mud.

Christopher launched himself toward the gun as a bullhorn screamed, "Let's have a little quiet. We're trying to shoot a war here."

F-Stop fell aside, his eyes fixed and staring.

Brewster landed on top of Christopher with a thud. The reporter's breath whooshed out. Even so, his mind shrieked at him to get the gun. His fingers locked on metal, scrabbled for the trigger guard. Then suddenly the Luger was gone, out of his grasp as Brewster knocked it away.

Christopher made another grab for it. But he was carrying Brewster's weight now, and that pressed him face-down into the mud. The reporter bucked and thrashed, anything to free his mouth and nose of the goo, anything to get a breath inside his burning lungs. But the bucking did no good.

In desperation, he began rocking from side to side. After a moment, his face came free for a brief instant, just long enough for him to suck in a lungful of sweet air.

He was thanking God when a stab of pain caused him to cry out, dissipating much of his precious oxygen. Brewster had shifted his attack to the reporter's wounded shoulder. Flames of pain burned all the way down his arm and out into his fingertips. Even the freshly flowing blood couldn't extinguish such a blaze of agony.

Still on top, Brewster slammed a second punch into the throbbing wound. Pain, bright and bursting, exploded behind Christopher's eyes, blinding him. Fear and agony sent him crazy. Yet part of him knew that he had to rid himself of Brewster's weight quickly before it could sap all strength.

Biting down on his own lip to steep himself in pain, Christopher ducked his head and rolled onto his bad shoulder. Again, flames licked at him, but he was ready for them this time. He kept rolling.

The maneuver caught Brewster by surprise. Christopher rolled free. But that freedom lasted only an instant before Christopher attacked. This time he landed on top, flailing blindly down at his enemy.

Brewster's answer was to jab his fingernails into the reporter's bloody shoulder.

Screaming through tears, Christopher lashed out with all the force he could muster. His fist made a satisfying thump as it landed on target. Suddenly Brewster's blows felt weaker.

Christopher swung at the man's throat. His fist struck dead-center.

Brewster gurgled. All air and fight went out of him, but

Christopher couldn't stop himself now. He lashed out again and again, for F-Stop, for Irma, for himself.

Finally, when he no longer had strength to lift his arms, he used his legs to lever himself from Brewster's limp body. Then the reporter sank, hands first, into the mud. For the first time, the goo felt cool and refreshing. He blinked to clear his eyes of mud.

Only then did he realize that Brewster was slowly curling into a fetal ball.

And that's when Susan fired the gun.

26

BALANCING A LARGE pizza carton on the palm of one hand, Christopher edged sideways into the news director's office, where he was greeted with a sharp hoot of derision.

"If you gain any more weight," Reisner hollered, "I'm going to start deducting so much a pound from your salary."

The reporter sat down carefully, spread the box on the news director's desk, then took a deep whiff, hoping to dull his mind with the smell of pepperoni and mushroom. As an afterthought, he offered a slice to Reisner.

Shuddering, the news director said, "It's only ten o'clock in the morning." With that he picked up his phone and ordered two coffees from his secretary.

"I'd prefer beer."

"Not during working hours."

"Who's working?"

"It's not the end of the world, Bobbo."

Christopher grimaced. The news director hadn't seen F-Stop's body, nor did he share the reporter's guilt for getting a friend killed.

Christopher sank his teeth into a slice of pizza. The crust was crisp, just the way he liked it. With his second bite, cheese stretched out into a long string that wrapped itself around his chin.

He remembered reading somewhere that after thirty-five food was better than sex. A bold-faced lie, he decided. Certainly the tomato sauce, good as it was, did nothing to dull his memory of Susan, or his bad feeling about F-Stop either, for that matter.

Christopher let out his new belt a notch, then helped himself to a second piece, chewing doggedly. Before he could move onto slice number three, Reisner said, "Okay, I surrender. I can tell by the look on your face that you're dying to tell me the details."

"You read the papers, didn't you?"

"I didn't read anything about a killer being caught."

"I had it on tape."

"Had?"

"Susan dumped the cassette in a mud puddle before I could do anything about it. You know what water does to tape. When we tried to play it, there was nothing left of Brewster's confession. Naturally Susan was afraid Wyn had implicated her." Christopher stared at the news director. "So just how are you going to play it on 'The Six O'Clock News' tonight, Herb?"

Reisner closed one eye, thinking. "Any way you want. It's your story."

Taking a mouthful, Christopher considered his options.

"Come on," Reisner snapped. "Out with it. I've got an appointment with Robin Flick in a few minutes."

With a sigh, the reporter loked up at the THINK MEAN sign. F-Stop's comment in spearmint still dotted the i.

Not much to leave behind, Christopher thought briefly, then realized that he was being foolish. F-Stop's true legacy had been on videotape, one destroyed by Susan, and one she didn't know existed. Unfortunately the second tape, which F-Stop had loaded into the camera and left running before joining Christopher in the mud, had been ambiguous.

"I've got nearly ten minutes of tape and it's not worth a damned thing," he told the news director.

Absently, Reisner began eating a slice of pizza.

"What I played for the police was Susan's denial to me that she knew anything about the killings. They didn't like it, especially after what I've told them, but they can't prove otherwise. Of course, they'd planned to use Franks against her by offering him immunity to testify. But immunity doesn't mean anything to a dead man."

Christopher snagged another slice of pizza, but it never

177

made it to his mouth. Memory regurgitated the NRS man's dead face and killed the reporter's appetite.

"They found Franks in the same garage where I'd seen him making it with Susan," Christopher said. "His car was still idling. Another convenient suicide doesn't go down well, but what can the police do? They think Brewster killed the man before meeting me on the back lot. But they're not about to say so without evidence. Besides, what good would it do?"

The reporter offered the remaining slice to Reisner, but the news director declined.

Christopher said, "There's really no doubt Wyn killed the man. Hell, Wyn's career would have been in his hands. And I don't think Brewster was about to risk blackmail a second time, not with New York within his grasp."

The reporter sighed. He was feeling no pain, thanks to a shot of novocaine. "And when they talked to Susan, she had an answer for everything. She now claims she shot Brewster to save my life. At that point on the videotape there's nothing to disprove it."

Christopher scooped up the pizza carton and crushed it into Reisner's waste basket. "I told them that she shot Brewster to keep him quiet about her part in the killings. But if I say any different from now on she can sue me for slander."

"And the police are just going to drop it?"

Christopher shrugged. "Without proof against Susan, they're content to call Franks a suicide and Brewster's death justifiable homicide. It not only clears the books for them, but comes as close to justice as they can get."

"All right, Bob. Now it's my turn to ask how you're going to play it on the news?"

Christopher's answer was interrupted by the arrival of Robin Flick.

By the time Robin was ready to leave Reisner's office, she had escaped the Sunday morning ghetto forever. To do it, she'd given up the title of producer. But Reisner, acting on Aarons's behalf, had assured her that being an associate producer on the news was far more prestigious than top dog on any religious throwaway.

"And what do you think?" she asked, turning to Christopher, who'd stayed behind at the news director's insistence.

"For someone like yourself," Christopher said honestly, "associate producer is just a stepping stone. There's no telling how far you can go."

Reisner's eye was rolling wildly but Christopher ignored it to ask him, "And just what will Robin's duties be, Herb?"

"That will be up to Al of course."

"Well then, why don't we go down the hall and ask him?"

Reisner made a fist and knuckled his bad eye with it. "I can guess what he has in mind."

"Come on," Robin said haughtily, catching Christopher by the hand. "We'll go see for ourselves."

As the reporter was trailing Robin out the door, Reisner called to him, "Don't forget. We need some kind of a wrap-up for the 'Six.' "

"I'll come up with something."

What Al Aarons had come up with was an electronic camera, complete with two stands of bright lights. All were aimed at the couch in his office.

"Are you getting ready to do an interview?" Robin asked.

To Christopher, the answer to that was perfectly obvious. Al Aarons wasn't the kind of man to learn from past indiscretions.

Ignoring the reporter, AA swept an arm around Robin's shoulder and said, "I have friends in the technical department." With his free hand he patted the camera. "This baby is set to run on automatic. All I have to do is flip this switch"—he demonstrated—"and we can make our own home movies."

"Reisner wants me to start work as soon as possible," Robin said.

"That's why you're here."

"What are my duties going to be?"

Aarons leered. "As soon as our dear friend Christopher leaves us alone, I'll show you."

27

Dr. Janice Owen had been promoted to chief of staff at "Emergency Hospital," a role offering her double the on-camera time. Such was the power of publicity at ABN.

"Not only that," Susan told Christopher, entertaining him in her new dressing room, "my agent says I've become a hot property overnight."

The reporter looked for a fire extinguisher, but saw only the trappings of success.

"They're talking about a movie of the week for me," she went on, "though the script hasn't been written yet. But they're thinking of calling it *The ABN Story*. Sort of a biography. I'll have to save your life all over again."

"Who's playing me?"

"They're hoping for a big name, someone with enough pull to ensure a theatrical release later on."

"Will you be convicted of murder in the movie?"

Susan smiled. "Are you here as a newsman?"

"There are no hidden mikes this time, if that's what you mean."

"An actress is always on stage. Her fans expect that. Besides, that's the only way to survive in this business."

"I'm not asking you to sign a confession. But I'd like to hear a better reason than the ratings for what you did."

"Ratings, publicity, it's all the same. You're famous too, you know. But the spotlight only stays on you for a little while. And you've got to shine while it's there."

She nodded at her own wisdom. "I'll tell you what, Bob. I'll put in a word for you with my agent. Maybe he can get you a role in the movie."

"I can only play myself."

"That's impossible. You know we need a star."

"I'm happy where I am." As he spoke the words, Christopher realized they were the truth, that he wasn't about to leave TV news.

"You can't expect me to be seen around town with a nobody, not when my career is ready to take off."

He sighed and closed his eyes, but he could still see her in his mind.

"That doesn't mean I can't see you once in a while on the side," she went on.

"Assignations in the ambulance?" he suggested, forcing his eyes back open.

"Why not? You're an interesting man. Not all that bad looking either. So there's no reason why we can't remain *close*."

Susan licked her lips and smiled sensuously, leaving no doubt as to what she had in mind. Looking at her, he realized that he still ached to have her. At the same time, the thought of touching her disgusted him.

Christopher headed for the dressing room door.

"You're the best ambulance chaser I ever had," she called after him.

He didn't trust his voice to reply.

28

A NEW STORM, bringing with it icy rain, was raising hell by the time Christopher left Stage C. The assignment desk beeped him, but he ignored the summons. He didn't have time to worry about natural disaster, not when he still had Irma on his mind.

He ran for the executive bungalow. There, with promises of free lunches and introductions to eligible jocks, he talked his way past Norma Lewis and into Brewster's office. The safe held a copy of Al Aarons's famous video tape. And the combination, Christopher remembered, was simple enough, Wyn Brewster's birthday.

Shaking fingers turned simplicity into a contest of will. Finally, however, the safe opened. For a moment, Christopher debated the advisability of playing the tape then and there. But he was kidding himself. He had to know, *now*.

After viewing the pornography from start to finish, he was none the wiser. The only familiar face to be seen belonged to Al Aarons.

Rewinding the cassette, the reporter wondered if Brewster had lied to him. If so, Christopher would never know the whole story.

With a sigh, he set the playback for slow motion and restarted the tape. The movie, twenty years old according to Aarons, was scratched and faded.

Two decades hadn't changed AA that much, the reporter decided. But the other face, distorted as it was by phony passion and bleached blond hair, Christopher would never have recognized. Even twenty years ago it hadn't been young, especially by comparison to her co-star. But in slo-mo, with the reporter's face pressed right against the screen, he could plainly see the St. Christopher medal around her neck.

Gusting wind caught his umbrella and turned it inside out. He hurled the mess at a trash barrel and started toward the news building. He still had to prepare an eyewitness account for "The Six O'Clock." Only tonight, lacking proof, he would have to edit out much of the truth. Sure, he knew what Irma had been in the past. And that she had been killed to keep from destroying her X-rated co-star's reputation and with it Brewster's plan to juggle the ratings. But that still left the reporter wondering about Irma's motives. Had she blackmailed only to feed her animals, only to help along her idea of St. Christopher? Christopher would never know for sure.

And what about Susan? She'd never confessed her guilt, not in so many words, even on the tape that had been destroyed. But the reporter didn't need that kind of proof. He'd seen her carrying out Brewster's instructions, seen the look on her face when she helped lure F-Stop to his death. Even so, Christopher would have to keep his mouth shut when he went on the air at six. Either that or commit slander.

Rain, verging on sleet, started him shaking beyond even what Susan had accomplished. He had to clench his teeth to keep them quiet.

Suddenly, he realized that he couldn't face Reisner and the newsroom crowd, not yet. He veered away from the building and hurried to his car. A ticket for parking illegally had been stuck on his windshield. When he switched on the wipers, the blades churned the paper into mush, which was exactly how he felt driving home.

Exhaustion threatened to overwhelm him the moment he stepped inside the house. The trek to the bedroom left him panting. But he still had breath enough to gasp at the new leak in the ceiling, from which water was cascading down onto his bed.

Christopher swore. Either a new raccoon had moved in or he'd done a sloppy job repairing the roof.

Then another explanation occurred to him. Maybe the raccoons in the garage had escaped. But when he checked, they were present and accounted for, hissing at him from behind overturned garbage cans.

He armed himself with a broom before venturing all the way into the garage to fetch shingles and nails. The stepladder was already in place from his last expedition.

In daylight, gray as it was, he spotted a bare patch of roof where the wind had been at work. But hammering half a dozen wooden shingles into place proved more difficult than he'd expected. The rain was blinding and his throbbing shoulder made each swing of the hammer a thrill.

By the time he finished, Christopher had a swollen finger to go along with the tremors rattling his entire body. He didn't bother returning tools to the garage, but headed straight for a hot bath, where he soaked his shakes away, while doing his best to keep his bandages dry. But he could do nothing to change his mood, to ease the feeling of depression that was threatening to engulf him.

Dried and dressed, he went to the phone and called the newsroom, leaving word with a secretary that he would be in soon. Then he decided to fix himself a drink. He was adding hot water to a half glass of whisky when he heard scrabbling from the garage.

"Damn." He'd forgotten to feed the raccoons, though they'd already helped themselves to a smorgasbord from the garbage cans.

Just as he was clamping a can of real tuna into the electric opener, Christopher shouted. The raccoons had given him an idea. Maybe there was justice in this world after all. He dumped the fish onto a paper plate and opened the connecting door between kitchen and garage.

"A going away present," he called and shoved the food at the animals.

Then the reporter retreated to the kitchen, where he

185

listened to them squeaking and squabbling over the tuna. A smile tugged at his lips. For an instant, the expression felt totally out of place, like laughter at a funeral. But then the smile grew into a grin.

He laughed all the way outside where, heedless of the rain, he opened the garage door. For a moment, the raccoons did nothing but blink at him, their nocturnal eyes unable to cope. Then they scampered to freedom.

Not much justice, he thought. But at least Susan was in for a series of very painful rabies shots.